United States of America 2020

ISBN:9798552509119

Imprint: Independently published

D1092509

MVFOL

thank you

Diana,

Thank you for
your support!

Best
Heorm

R Baskerville Hearon

Season II Season

what goes around comes around

Acknowledgments

My sincerest thoughts and appreciation goes to everyone who enjoyed reading my first suspenseful novella, "Seasons." My readers expressed that they loved the first of this trilogy only to be left hanging at the end. The first-time putting thoughts to paper for everyone to read is when you are truly free. Self-expression can be the most vulnerable action one can do. You never know how far you should take things. Sometimes our most profound thoughts can be so opposite of how others think; it makes us suppress instead of express. The people who advised me not to be afraid to go deeper telling my stories get the credit for my uninhibited expressions.

Season II Season picks up where Seasons left off and has even more suspenseful surprises with new and exciting characters that will leave you wanting even more. My request is if you enjoy this one as much as the first, then please pass it on to a loved one or friend, so they can feel as delighted as you are reading as I did writing it. The beginning stories of; Leilani, Art, and Veronica's lives took readers on a tailspin of excitement and intrigue as they traveled all over the world, enjoying the finer things in life. A life of not having a care in the world is only a fantasy to most of us but can also change in the blink of an eye. If you don't believe in Karma, good or bad, then maybe this trilogy will change your mind.

As promised, Season 11 Season will take its readers on an even more suspenseful journey with additional characters added to their circle. Added are the much-needed backstories of each character, explaining why they are the way they are. The sheer enticement of unpredictability is something I crave and will always write about in my novellas. If you see your name in any of the characters I've created, please accept it as nothing more than a compliment. None of the stories I write about are factual. These stories I write are from my vivid imagination and nothing more. As always, I hope you enjoy every character that I continue to add, making these novellas come to life.

After reading this book, if you purchased it on Amazon, please take a moment to write a review. It's the best way to get the word out to other readers. Thank you in advance.

These are some of my favorite songs I listen to before, during, and after I write; u move, I move, Let's all get right, real big, higher, late nights and early mornings, losing, nonstop, no guidance, you stay, i'm not ok, get you, whatever you need, hard place, black bonnie, losing, double up, the matrimony, lightning and thunder, I wanna be with you, sue me, moments, blue dream. the weekend, slide, on the way, just us, sativa, gonna love me, the weather, best i ever had, every kind of way, come over, my song, no love, shut it down, gold roses, don't want you, drunk texting, hello, girls need love, could have been, nobody, marathon, new balance, shot clock, magic hour, rather be hurt, shut it down, bigger than life, nonstop, bed peace, love me like that, triggered, p*$$y fairy (OTW), Summer 2020.

Chapter One

Leilani

As fireworks light the sky, music, hugs, kisses under the mistletoe, and great food at the stroke of midnight is happening worldwide. Leilani sits quietly on her balcony, watching the beautiful streams of colorful lights exploding in the Las Vegas sky. Eagerly anticipating this new year, she feels the forceful thump growing inside her belly due in six short weeks. Her reflection of the past eight months has been nothing short of eventful, but her focus is solely on the arrival of her bundle of joy. Never thinking she would ever have a child of her own, she feels blessed and sad at the same time. Entering the world of motherhood alone leaves her feeling sad but determined.

Just months earlier, after grieving the loss of Art, Leilani took a trip to the Bayou of Louisiana at the end of summer, where her father's family all live. She wanted to be better acquainted and thought it would be a good idea to bring them inside her world. She arrived in the city of Kenner, ten miles outside of New Orleans in Jefferson Parish. Her taxi drives slowly down the long driveway of connecting, centuries-old oak trees unveiling a beautiful two-story Plantation style home-centered by one acre of land. Her beautiful Creole family range from toddlers to grandparents in their late nineties, including uncles, aunts, and cousins that she has never met before this day. With loving, hospitable southern charm, she is welcomed with open arms the moment she walked in.

As she entered through the tall double doors of this massive mansion, there is a buzz of excitement in the air as they know she is pregnant. She observes beautiful paintings on walls hanging right up to the high ceilings. Brilliant crystal chandeliers are in every room as she walks through on hardwood floors. Her grandparents' classic southern style home is the primary place the family gathers playing Zydeco music, dancing, laughing, drinking, and, most of all, eating outstanding traditional Creole cuisine.

The women, young and old, are gorgeous, the men are handsome, and all the kids are just beautiful. Her younger cousin Giselle quickly grabs her hand, leading through the house to the home's main sitting area to meet the family's elders. Sitting together, her grandparents are old, but she can see her dad in both their faces. Her old school grandparents spoke Creole, but Leilani, didn't fully understand them, so Giselle interpreted what they said and took her around to meet everyone else. There were at least fifty people inside the house, and Leilani loved it. Growing up as an only child in Cali, it was always just she and her mom.

An array of classic Creole dishes sit on three main tables. Crawfish étouffee, red beans & dirty rice, gumbo, andouille jambalaya, shrimp & oyster po'boys, shrimp boil, fried chicken, fried pork chops, collard greens, chicken Creole, fried catfish, King crab legs, potato salad, chicken fricassee, Oxtail stew, grits crawfish, and crab cakes, and hot water cornbread are on

2

one table. Pralines, Bourbon bread pudding, sweet potato and pecan pies, cheesecakes, and Crème Brulée are on another table. The plates, cutlery, napkins, and drinks are on the third table, and now that she is here, everyone grabs a plate and digs in. She tried to eat a little bit of everything until she couldn't eat another bite. Being with her Louisiana family happy and cheerfully eating great food with little kids running around laughing as adults tell stories and jokes, is just what she needs. Looking at all the beautiful pictures and engaging with her family made her think about Art. They all expressed their condolences regarding Art's passing and were sad for her, but we're happy she was having a baby.

Most of her cousins were her same age, so she felt comfortable hanging out with them. Her aunts and uncles told funny stories and showed her lots of pictures of her dad growing up in the Bayou, and she was grateful because her mom never had any. All her dad's brothers and sisters looked just alike as children, but they pointed her dad out in each photo. He was the oldest son of six siblings and was the only one who moved out of Louisiana. After sunset, her cousins suggested they go into New Orleans, "The Big Easy" to hang out and enjoy the city. About a dozen cousins jumped in several cars and took Leilani into the city. As they walk down the French Quarter's cobblestone streets, Leilani spotted a curious looking Mambo Voodoo Priestess salon storefront. Wondering about her fate, she stepped inside.

This explosive and colorful Louisiana history has scented candles, dried flowers, colorful fabrics on the ceilings, flags, tapestries, feathered masks, and old pictures covering every wall. On one end of the table sat a throne-like chair where the Priestess sits and one multicolored wood chair for the patron to sit on. Leilani's loose clothing camouflaged her pregnancy, so the Priestess could not tell she is pregnant. The woman asks for Leilani's hands so she can feel her energy. As Leilani lays her hand on the Priestesses hand, she gives her a one-hundred-dollar bill. The Priestess smiles, bows her head, and gives thanks to her for more than a proper payment. After a few moments of meditating and reading her energy, what came out of the Priestess's mouth to Leilani blows her away. Leilani's aura of joy, happiness, wealth, grief, and death is apparent to the Priestess.

She talked about two recent losses; one financial and the other a close loved one, but not to worry because her blessing is on the way! Wow, Leilani thought; she kept quiet as the Priestess continued with her insight. She went on to say, "Someone robbed you of something that is rightfully yours, and it would be in your best interest to seek that which is yours." She said, *"You need to do this for your child."* Perplexed, Leilani said, "but I do not have any children." The woman looked at her boldly and said, "but you will soon. I see a love child in your near future". The woman also said, "what is for you is clearly in writing. Your life will continue to be unsettled until you take heed, so pay attention". Just then, her cousins stepped inside to check on her. Leilani turned to them, graciously thanked the Priestess, and left. Leilani rejoined her cousins as they all continue walking down the streets of New Orleans.

As Leilani reconnects with her cousins laughing and having fun in the French Quarter, she feels disconcerted by what the Priestess said. Brushing it off for now, she redirects her attention back to her cousins and enjoys the rest of the fun in the city. On the way back to the house, Leilani was quiet and deep in thought. Her emotions are full, and her ideas are mostly of Art. Before leaving the next day, she took pictures with everyone in her family, exchanged numbers, bid them farewell, and promised to stay connected. Just before getting in her taxi headed for the airport, her cousin Giselle who recently graduated from college, asked if she could come to visit sometime soon to help her with the baby and to experience Vegas. "Sure, of course, call me anytime." With that said, she hugged her, got in the taxi, and left for the airport for the flight home.

Returning to Vegas after experiencing the intense humidity of Louisiana, the triple digits of September slowly begin to force the temperature to drop for the upcoming Fall and winter seasons. Her studio apartment is cute, but it is not sufficient for a baby whose arrival is just a mere five months away, so before she traveled to Louisiana, she hired a realtor to find her a house. On her computer, she opens several emails from her agent and eagerly reads them. "*Hi Leilani, I found the perfect home with all your specifications, so please call me as soon as you get this email. Here are the pics below*". As Leilani viewed all the pics of the house, she loved it and thought, *yes, she's right; it's perfect*, so Leilani replied, "*I agree, it's lovely, let's do a walkthrough.*"

The next day, Leilani met with her Realtor at the new house, and just like the pictures, the home is gorgeous and perfect in every way. She submitted a cash offer, they accepted it, and she had a two-week escrow. Leilani now has the arduous task of moving. She has been living in her small but quaint apartment for over ten years, and even though she was rarely there, her whole life was there. Happy to be a homeowner, Leilani thought about all the times of having to move every year growing up for one reason or another. Times were always hard for them, and she promised one day, she would never have to worry about *moving under duress* ever again.

The next day, Leilani drove to the Mother's Nest to catch up with the staff and see how everything is going. The center is full of stable residents, and everything is running smoothly, so it is one less concern. Her staff is happy to see her, and she shows them the pics she took and told them all about her Creole family from her dad's side in Louisiana. She has a lot on her plate now, needing to move, and with the baby on the way, she also needs to decide what she wants to do with *B.S.G.* Santa Monica.

So far, her first trimester has been uneventful, with no morning sickness or spotting, but still being cautious, she wants to do everything right so she can get through her second and third trimester and delivery. She has a doctor's appointment to check everything and learn the gender of the baby from a 3-D sonogram. While in the waiting room of her Doctors office, Leilani receives a text message from her cousin Tony from New Orleans. He told her he's planning to relocate to Vegas because the restaurant where he works has a location there. Tony is a great cook, and his resume stands tall. Delighted to hear from him and thinking it is a good idea to have family around, she immediately responds to his text and tells him to call her as soon as he arrives in town.

The nurse calls her into the room and gets her set up for the ultrasound. She takes Leilani's vitals and begins to check all the major organs and heartbeat of the baby. As her Doctor walks in, she greets Leilani and asks how she feels. The nurse has a challenge getting the right angle to tell the baby's gender, but she keeps at it until the Doctor expresses concern and suggests taking over. Nervous, Leilani asks if everything is ok. The Doctor tells Leilani, "It's ok; sometimes babies aren't in the mood to reveal themselves and not to worry." With every stroke of the probe, Leilani notices the baby's heartbeat sounds are getting softer and lighter. Afraid, she asks again if everything is ok. Now the Doctor has the perfect view to see the baby's gender. "Ok, she said, would you like to know the sex of the baby"? Yes, Leilani replied. "Ok, you're having a girl, and she's due to arrive around Valentines' day"! Leilani closed her eyes and smiled. *A girl, she thought, what a wonderful surprise.* Now she needs to think about naming her little bundle of joy.

Leilani is excited about having a girl but could not help but think about the baby she lost years ago when she was with Paul. Shifting her thoughts, she mentally prepares for her big move. Tony sends her another text, telling her he will be in Vegas within the week. She looks around her apartment to see what she wants to keep. Her neighbor next door is a sweet, older retired lady on a fixed income, and Leilani told her to take whatever she wants. That way, she won't have to pack so much, and she can buy everything new and start fresh. They chatted, and Leilani told her about her trip to see her dad's family in Louisiana and showed her the pictures. Just as she thought, her neighbor wanted most of her stuff, so she gladly gave her whatever she wanted. Her neighbor was grateful and wished Leilani well.

Tony's flight arrived in Vegas the following Thursday evening, and Leilani picked him up from the airport right on time. He has never been to Vegas but has seen lots of tv commercials of the sin city lifestyle, so he is excited. She took the long way home so he could get a glimpse of the city, and she promised to take him out on the town officially later. Leilani's house will be ready to move into on Saturday, so Tony's decision to relocate is quintessential. He's a big teddy bear, standing six foot four, weighing about two hundred and fifty pounds, with a heart of gold. Her place is small, so he crashed on the couch for the night. The next morning, he moved everything her neighbor wanted over to her apartment and helped Leilani pack the rest to take over to the new house.

Moving day has arrived, and Leilani's four thousand square foot home is perfect with five bedrooms, five and a half baths, an office, and a large backyard. She and the baby will live there comfortably and have plenty of room for guests and entertaining. Furniture delivery trucks pull up one after the other, and she and Tony start to set things up. "This is a beautiful house, Cousin. You have it going on, girl", Tony told her as he looks around. The kitchen is any cooks dream with top of the line Viking appliances, and of course, Tony wants to break it in, so he gladly volunteers to cook their first meal. The neighbors directly across the street saw all the delivery vans, so they came over, rang the bell to welcome them to the neighborhood. Tony answered the door, they politely introduced themselves, and he invited them in. "Leilani, your neighbors are here," Tony shouted, and Leilani came downstairs from the nursery to greet them. Larry and Carol, a friendly, young couple, are also expecting a baby, but she is a month further along than Leilani, due in January. Immediately, they are mesmerized at the sight of the house, complimenting her on how beautiful everything is, so Leilani offers to give them a tour since it's so different from theirs. Leilani is excited to see that Carol is also pregnant, and the two become fast friends and hang out regularly over the next months.

Leilani settled into her new home decorating it in her favorite modern Boho/Feng Shui style. The bright and warm eclectic colors make her feel the most comfortable and, at the same time, reduces her stress. She and Carol spent time together quite a bit, going to lunches and shopping for baby things or just having fun together as girls. Leilani invited Larry and Carol and a few other friends over for a Thanksgiving feast, and Tony invited a friend from work as well. She and Tony did their thing in the kitchen, and everyone felt like royals and were glad they said yes to the invitation. After everyone left, Leilani and Tony woke up to sirens and blaring red lights just past midnight. They looked out the front window and saw an ambulance and a fire truck at Larry and Carol's house. Oh no, Leilani shouted! She and Tony rushed out to see if they were ok. Just then, the E.M.T.'s brought Carol out on a stretcher and put her into the ambulance.

Leilani, saddened to see this, asked one of the medics what happened, but he just ignored her and focused on something else. She looked at Larry, obviously in shock and stressed, then she asked him what happened. He said Carol slipped and fell as he climbed into the ambulance with her. Leilani asked him to please keep her posted as the ambulance drove away. A few hours later, Larry called Leilani and said she fractured her arm and ankle, will need to be on bed rest and may have to stay in the hospital until the baby is born. Wow, Leilani thought, it's sad for her having to be in a hospital instead of at home.

The next day, Leilani went to the hospital to see and hopefully cheer Carol up with her favorite Jamba juice. Shocked to see her all banged up lying there, Leilani asked what happened. Carol told her she and Larry were arguing, and in the heat of the argument, she tripped and fell down the stairs! Carol also said *he might have pushed her.* Leilani could not believe what she was hearing and suddenly became afraid for Carol. Attempting to change the subject, Leilani told her to concentrate on getting better for the baby. Reflecting, Leilani never really saw the two of them being lovey-dovey with each other and never saw them kiss or display any genuine affection for each other, which she always thought was strange.

The following day, the contractor laid the concrete slab for the backyard patio. A few days later, his crew returned to build a lighted pergola with two ceiling fans and installed an eight-speaker sound system. Planted were; sod, fruit trees, Birds of Paradise, a dozen rose bushes, four trees, pink and gold Bougainvillea, white jasmine vines, and colorful African

Gazania's interweaved with mint as ground cover. Looking around, everything in her backyard came out better than expected, so she is pleased.

Although Art's backyard is four times larger, she loves hers because it's hers. As the sun begins to set, she sits on her new patio, enjoys the view of her beautiful backyard while listening to Jhene Aiko, thinking about what else she wants to do before the baby arrives. She gets a text from her cousin Giselle, Tony's younger sister, who also wants to come out to Vegas to help with the baby, and of course, Leilani said yes. With Christmas being just around the corner, Leilani is usually in a festive mood, but she feels unsettled about Carol. Looking out front across the street and was shocked to see a For Rent sign in their yard. She also notices a familiar car parked in their driveway, so she continues to look.

Moments later, out walks Veronica and gets into the car. Shocked, Leilani realizes the reason the car looked familiar was that its Arts car. Wow, she thought, her heart skips a beat, considering how she never wanted to see Veronica again. Her first instinct was to run outside and say something but watched her instead. With her heart racing feeling like it was going to jump out of her chest, she wondered how Veronica knew Carol and Larry and why she was even there. As a million and one things ran through her mind, she decided to keep a mental note of it and see if she could get some answers from Carol instead of approaching Larry about it.

The next day Leilani went to the hospital to revisit Carol. She recalled the two talking about their family dynamics and remembered Carol seldom spoke personably about their baby. The two ladies chatted, then

11

Leilani told her she's having a challenge deciding what to name her baby. Sensing Carol's disinterest, Leilani asked if she was ok. With tears, Carol broke down and divulged that it's not her baby and that she is a surrogate carrying the baby for Larry's "rich" friend. Wanting her to go on with more details, Leilani responded supportively, saying she thinks being a surrogate is impressive.

Carol told Leilani about the whole surrogate process, adding that his "rich" friend has lots of money, but because she travels so extensively, she doesn't have the time to carry a baby of her own. She also told Leilani that his friend paid them $100K, which is three times the average amount, and set them up in that house to be comfortable, but more importantly, close by her, which made her more comfortable. Hoping Carol would mention her name, she went on to say the woman found them online and continued to drop little tidbits and hints about her. Finally, Carol mentions her name, saying, "But Veronica is excited about the baby." Boom! Leilani knew it was her but is surprised about Veronica having a baby as well.

Late evening on Christmas eve, Leilani and Tony arrive at the airport to pick up Giselle. They hugged each other, and Tony loaded her luggage in the trunk. Giselle's first time traveling to Vegas, her eyes are fixated on all the lights and beautiful casinos as they travel to Leilani's house. Once they arrive, Leilani gave her a quick tour and then led Giselle to her room. "Wow, your house is beautiful, Leilani," Giselle said. "Thank you, make yourself at home; you're welcome to stay here for as long as you like." With beautiful Christmas décor inside and out, including a ten-foot, fully decorated Christmas tree with lots of beautifully wrapped gifts underneath, Giselle hands her baby gifts from the family to add to the mountain of others. Thank you, Leilani said. The two cousins talked for a while, then Tony chimed in, "Hey ladies, today has been a long day, so I am going to bed, have a good night. I will see you in the morning."

Early Christmas morning, Leilani and Tony begin to prepare breakfast as holiday music softly plays throughout the house. After smelling the food, Giselle wakes up and walks downstairs to join them. After breakfast, they cleaned up and went into the front room to open presents from under the tree. She shipped the Christmas gifts for her B.S.G. staff in Santa Monica about a week ago. Next, they head over to the center for a few hours. When they arrive at the center, Tony and Giselle look all around and are impressed to see how everything looks. The families are in the facility's large kitchen and dining area, enjoying the celebration. While everyone is eating, Tony and a few employees go to the back storage shed to retrieve all the kids' bikes.

The Christmas holiday season is the biggest celebration of the year at the center, and Leilani goes all out for the families. With hundreds of thousands of dollars donated from corporate sponsors throughout the year to help keep the facility running well, extra contributions flood in during this time of year. Every child receives a bike, three toys, a pair of shoes, a coat, and the moms get a $200 gift card. Leilani remembers getting little to nothing on Christmas day growing up, simply because her mother didn't have the money. These moms at the center also have limited incomes, so this is the time of year Leilani makes sure they enjoy the holiday season, knowing that they will always remember it. While the kids enjoy opening their gifts, Leilani looks on with a joyful heart, feeling blessed to be able to make it all happen.

As the culinary staff prepares the holiday dinner of; turkey, ham, fried chicken, dressing with gravy, vegetables, mac & cheese, candied yams, and a host of delicious desserts and beverages, the incredible aromas fill the room. With so much excitement all around, Giselle looks at everything going on; touched by Leilani's generous philanthropy, she is glad to be here experiencing it all.

On the way home, they stopped by the Wynn as Leilani does every year to enjoy the annual Christmas display. Tony and Giselle have never seen such an impressive Christmas display, and they love everything they see. It is truly a sight to see, and they take it all in. As the year winds down to an end, Leilani reflects on what has happened over the past year. She has a lot to be grateful for and feels blessed in so many ways.

Chapter Two

A Valentine Special

This five-star, oceanfront, penthouse suite filled with exotic floral arrangements peaks her senses. On cold marble floors, she walks along a path of red and yellow rose petals leading to the bedroom with a bottle of Dom Pérignon champagne on ice. Delectable chocolates are on the pillows with more rose petals on the bed. Just a few steps away in the bathroom is a fragrant bubble bath drawn as soft music plays. As she takes in the pleasantries of this night of romance, her heart is thrilled. She slowly undresses and slides into the tub to enjoy the relaxing bath, and he begins to recite this classic poem as he pours her a glass of champagne.

If I were the water of your bath
I would surround you with mellow warmth, liquid love like frolicking,
childish waves on the sandy shore
I would dash and break upon the firmness of your body to engulf and
moisten the places I dream of
If I were the water of your bath,
being liquid; I would memorize each muscle and take your
shape, molding to your every curve and your every indentation.
I would roll on, over, and off your satin skin
If I were the water of your bath, I would send part of me
to gather in the recess of your navel where my temperature would rise to
match yours
and like plants of the sea, I would move your body hairs

in and out with the tide created by your movements
playfully I would slosh against your thighs and become very intimate
with your nature
If I were the water of your bath, I would cleanse you as my ancestors of
the Nile & Congo cleansed our ancestors
but even more when you leave me and pull the plug, I would defy the
natural order of things and stay and
wait for your naked return

He encourages her to enjoy the bubble bath and champagne as he showers and then waits for her in the bedroom. After finishing her luxurious bath, she joins him lying on the bed with the rose petals, now spelling the words "Marry me." In his hand is a blue Tiffany box. Overjoyed with all the romance he set up for her, she jumps into his arms and slowly opens the box. Inside is a beautiful five-carat, brilliant cut, solitaire diamond engagement ring. As they gaze into each other's eyes, he gently puts the ring on her finger and asks, "Will you be my wife?" She immediately says yes, and he smiles.

He holds her face with both his hands as they passionately kiss, then he moves his hands to the back of her neck and firmly grabs her long and curly locs. His kisses glide down to her neck, arousing her as she begins to moan. He gently lays her down on the bed and continues to kiss her down to her special place. Like a sweet and delicate flower, he opens her lips in search of her hidden pearl and lavishly licks it as it slowly rises from its hood. He licks long and slow like soft-serve ice cream, not missing a drop. His thick and soft lips latch on to her pearl as he applies just the right amount of suction, devouring her like a juicy summer peach. He slips one finger inside and upward, making come hither motions reaching her G-spot while inserting his other finger in her ass. He slowly goes in and out until she explodes as he sucks all her sweet, orgasmic nectar seeping out. They flip positions with her now on top. She goes up and down his shaft, around the head, sucking with her full mouth until he cums. Still erect, he immediately thrusts into her soft wetness again as they rock the bed until the dark blanket of stars dominate the fading sunset and fell asleep. The next morning as the light of the sun forces its way through their window, reflecting the glistening waters of the Atlantic Ocean, Veronica awakes to her fiancé Charles sleeping peacefully beside her. She is in love with this man and cannot imagine her life without him.

They have been together for eight years, and she is excited about finally getting married. She met Charles when she was in college, and he was just two years older. Young and ready to make their mark, they have mutual goals and dreams to have a good life. While she crammed for finals obtaining her undergraduate degree, he held down two jobs. He was a bouncer at Sapphire Gentlemen's Club at night, and during the day, he sold cars at a high-end luxury car dealership. Both were very attracted to each other; the two grew closer and began to date. As a trained bodyguard, Charles stands tall, looks quite intimidating, and is easy on the eye. He towers over Veronica's tiny and petite frame, and his fearless and confident demeanor always makes her feel safe.

During that time, Veronica had been living in Art's guesthouse for about a year. She felt having a driver/security guard would be a great idea, so she suggested Charles for the position. Because Veronica recommended him, Art hired him without hesitation and paid him well. Charles continued to sell the high-end cars and occasionally worked a few nights at the club just for fun. Because Charles has connections with high-end vehicles, Art established relationships to privately purchase all his cars and have them delivered to the house. Art purchased a brand-new Bentley and a Range Rover through Charles, and he already had a Mercedes two-door coupe and a medium-sized pickup truck. Art loved having Charles drive him around the city because it allowed him to drink and party worry-free, plus he felt protected since he is a trained bodyguard.

After Veronica graduated from college, during the first few years of them dating, she suffered several miscarriages, leaving her feeling discouraged about being pregnant. After so many, both heartbroken decided to put off having kids for a while, so she focused on getting her master's degree. They were very private about their relationship because she didn't think Art needed to know they saw each other. Hiding their love for each other over the years became problematic and was sometimes daunting because even though they were adults, they felt like two kids trying to beat curfew while seeing each other at Art's guesthouse. They worked at his house doing their prospective jobs during the day, maintaining a professional, business relationship. As life would have it, after a few years, Veronica no longer able to hold it in; she told Art that they were a couple, and he was ok with Charles moving into the guesthouse with her. Art liked having them close, and it made him feel like they were family even though they weren't in the main house with him.

Looking at Charles and Veronica, the two could not be more opposite, but they have similar personalities. Both observers of people, they are noticeably quiet and reserved. The two of them enjoyed each other's company so much that even when home smoking weed and just kicking it, doing nothing but listening to music, they still felt like nothing else was needed. They were never bored; their vibe has always been chill, no highs, and no lows, only chill to the fullest. Expressing big dreams and goals to each other, they forever talked about plans to do something big someday. Deep down, both of them were hungry not to be ordinary, but to be extraordinary and stand out even if in the background. Charles was the first of everything for Veronica. She trusted and believed in him implicitly.

Veronica, being witty, direct, and concise, Charles is more laid back, somewhat reserved, and likes to go with the flow. With her savvy business sense and his street-smart hustle mentality, they are a winning team. Charles is quite the connoisseur of weed and is an expert on just about everything there is to know about it. Veronica not so much, but once he showed her the profitable projections of growing, harvesting, and packaging cannabis, she convinced Art to invest. Art paid her well, and every time she helped him make substantial investments, he rewarded her with bonuses, which kept her on her toes, and her bank account stayed full. For a young woman in her early twenties, she was leaps and bounds ahead of her college friends who were out there pounding the pavement trying to secure their first real professional jobs.

Charles grew up as a Navy brat, born in St. David's Island in Bermuda, a British territory of the Caribbean Islands. His dad, now deceased, was a very tall and masculine Black man from Detroit. After joining the Navy, he met his mom, a white Island native from Barbados, during his deployment. Charles grew up in a family that expressed love often and thinks about how his parents, aunts, uncles, and cousins show their love every time he visits. His mother still lives in Barbados, so he travels there as often as he can. At the age of eleven, his family moved to Key West, Florida, while attending middle school. They relocated to San Diego, California, where he attended high school. Charles was a wide receiver at UNLV but suffered a knee injury causing him to lose an NFL career.

Veronica was born in Cleveland, Ohio, on the wrong side of the tracks near Imperial avenue to a Korean mother and Black father. Her mother, a tailor for a textile company, had a young teenage daughter when she met her dad, and within a few years, Veronica was born. Her dad, a taxi driver, never married her mom, although she believed they loved each other. Veronica's older sister, full Korean, hung out with the neighborhood kids and was found to be promiscuous with the boys. Her mom communicated in Korean to her sister often. Still, Veronica's dad insisted that she only speak English whenever he was present, so Veronica only knew a few Korean words and phrases here and there. Her sister became pregnant during her last year of high school, and her mom was quite upset, especially since she refused to tell her who the dad was. When the baby was

20

born, everyone could see that the dad was black. He was a cute little boy, and Veronica played with him like he was a little doll.

One afternoon, her mom came home early, and just before walking in the house, she overheard her dad and sister arguing. Her dad said, "Look; if that's my baby, I need to know!" Her mom could not believe her ears. She rushed inside and started yelling and screaming at the top of her lungs. "How dare you!" She shouted at Veronica's dad, and then she turned to her daughter and slapped her right on the face, almost knocking her down to the floor. Her mom kicked and screamed at her dad, fighting into the kitchen, and her sister ran up the stairs. Her mom grabbed a knife and attempted to stab her dad, but she just grazed him on the forearm. While breaking dishes along the way, her mom stepped on a piece of broken glass and cut her foot. Because of their loud yelling and shouting, the neighbors called the police. When the police arrived, what Veronica remembers most about that day was her sister and the baby left, her dad left, her mom went to the hospital, and social services put her in the foster care system, where she remained over the next twelve years.

Veronica was born into a home where she seldom heard the words "I love you" and never heard them at any of the families she lived with over the years. Social services had a strict placement plan for Veronica because after they learned her dad was having sex with her half-sister, Veronica got removed for safety. Her sister took the baby, moved out of state, and Veronica never saw them again. She was placed with many different families every year. She lived with several black families, then with a few white

21

families and one Hispanic family during the first six years. She missed her parents, sister, and nephew, but she gave up hope in ever seeing them again as the years passed. Her mother ultimately relinquished her rights and lost custody permanently, so Veronica eventually moved on mentally. Most of the homes she lived in were poor struggling families who fostered children because they needed the money, so she always knew she was merely a paycheck. Veronica had to fight over food, fight over clothes, fight kids and felt hated every day. She still had to share a bedroom, sleeping on either a twin or a bunkbed with many other children, and she never had any privacy. She lived in so many homes, making friends was difficult because she enrolled in a new school every year.

By age fifteen, as Veronica enrolled in high school, she was placed with a lovely Jewish family until she graduated, which was the best home of all. The Schwartz family lived in a three thousand square foot, two-story brick home with a pool, a big backyard, and lots of bath and bedrooms. She shared a room with their sixteen-year-old daughter as their oldest daughter prepared to leave for college. They also had two boys who shared a bedroom and bath, and the two younger foster kids were girls who had a bedroom and bath as well. They even had a vacation home in Florida that they all traveled to every summer for two weeks. A successful businessman, Papa Abba owns six gas stations throughout the city. His wife, who she calls Ema, which means "mom" in Hebrew, was a stay at home housewife who loves children, so after she could no longer conceive and feeling like an empty nester, Papa Abba agreed they could have as many foster kids as she wanted. Every chance Papa Abba got, he taught Veronica about finances and how to make money grow. She worked at his gas stations and learned how profitable businesses succeed, so she majored in Business when she attended college.

Still relaxing, room service delivers a lovely breakfast spread of fresh-cut fruits, Killer Dave's Good Seed avocado toast, bacon, sausage, scrambled eggs, juice, and coffee. She gently kisses his face to wake him. They eat in bed and discuss their wedding plans. Just then, a text comes in from Larry saying that although it's early, and the baby wasn't due until the end of January, Carol is in labor and will have the baby soon. Veronica immediately jumps up in a panic and tells Charles they need to go because the baby is coming. They both frantically pack their suitcases, and Veronica calls the pilot to meet them at the airport to get them back to Vegas. Their flight will take at least three hours, but Veronica was grateful to have the private jet and not wait for a commercial flight.

Once they land in Vegas, they immediately Uber over to the hospital, but when they arrived at the room, the baby was already in the bassinette next to Carol with Larry sitting in a corner chair looking on. Veronica apologizes for not coming in time for the birth but happy to be there now. She is a beautiful baby girl, weighing in at five pounds, six ounces, and they named her Alayna Chermaine. Carol had a c-section and had to remain in the hospital for at least another three days. The baby checks out fine, so she will be ready to go home to Veronica and Charles on that day as well. Veronica cannot take her eyes off the baby and is excited about finally being a mom. After losing so many babies in the past, it's a dream come true for her, and Charles is happy to be a dad.

It's day three, and Veronica is excited the baby is ready to come home with her and Charles. They thanked Larry and Carol, and they are anxious to get home, so she gives them plane tickets and sends them on their way. Parenthood is a new adventure for Veronica and Charles, so they take it all in with both hands and give it all they have. Each week they are presented with a new challenge but take it like champs, but their biggest one was when the baby got her days and nights mixed up for several weeks. Veronica changed formulas a couple of times as well as the brand of diapers due to allergic reactions. Caring for the baby was a little harder than she expected, so Charles noticing her struggles, he suggests that they hire a live-in babysitter to help. Refusing, Veronica insists on handling it. By week four, Veronica is exhausted from not getting any sleep, and again Charles reminds her that she can always get help. He helps to care for the baby, but Veronica promises to get professional help soon. Changing the subject, she went to the office, tackled the bills, and got on the computer to start looking for a Nanny. The three hundred-thousand-dollar hospital bill arrives. Shaking her head, she writes the check and mails it off.

On February thirteenth, late in the afternoon, Leilani feels contractions about five minutes apart, so Tony and Giselle take her to the hospital. The maternity staff gets her all prepared in the room, and she labors until just after midnight. As the baby crowns, the nurse told her to bear down and push, and out comes the baby, slowly but surely. The entire maternity staff is all excited as they welcome the first Valentine baby of the day. Arabella Love Graziani, born seven pounds, seven ounces, twenty-one inches long, and favors Art, having bright blue eyes. She is perfect and beautiful in every way, and Leilani cries tears of joy and sadness. She wishes so much that Art and Philippe were here to see her, but she is glad to have her cousins to share in this joyous occasion.

Charles made plans to spend a romantic Valentine evening with Veronica at home. He bought her a lovely diamond necklace with a matching bracelet, and he had a beautiful flower arrangement and a box of dark chocolates delivered. He also arranged for a Private Chef to prepare a nice steak and lobster dinner. The Chef promptly arrived, around five pm. He quickly prepared the food, served it to them, cleaned up, and left them with the dinner and dessert. As they ate, Charles presented her with the gifts one by one. Veronica felt terrible and apologized because she's been so busy with the baby, she didn't even realize it was Valentine's day. "No worries, he said, let's just enjoy this day." The meal was perfect, and after dinner, they enjoyed the dessert, smoked a blunt, and drank a bottle of wine. Content from eating that delicious meal and drinking the wine, they are both exhausted and doze off on the sofa.

Veronica suddenly wakes up, and the room is dark. She looks over at the baby monitor and notices her room is also dark. Veronica looked at the clock and saw that it's after eleven o'clock! Frantic, she rushed up to the baby's room, and just a moment later, Charles wakes up to her horrific and agonizing screams. He runs upstairs and finds Veronica standing next to the crib, sobbing profusely. Their baby girl is lying in the crib blue, cold to the touch, and stiff. Charles calls 911, and when the paramedics arrived, they ask what's her name and how old she is. "She's only six weeks," Veronica tearfully shouted. They rush over to the crib and find the baby lifeless, and there is nothing they can do. Alayna Chermaine's official cause of death was SIDS. Veronica was devastated, sobbing uncontrollably and unable to talk for several days, so Charles took over to make the memorial arrangements. Veronica is still heartbroken and remains silent.

Veronica tries to get her mind back to normal, but she is too overwhelmed with grief, and Charles's efforts to comfort her doesn't seem to work. He redecorated the baby's room into a guest room to avoid the obvious. Feeling awkward, Charles feels it's best not to talk about the baby. As the weeks turn into months, the strain is taking its toll on their relationship, so before they start to drift apart, he suggests that they take a trip to get away for a change of scenery. His first thought is to take her home to the Caribbean, but as depressed as she is, being around his family may not be such a good idea. Charles suggests they should go to Maui since they've never been there. She agreed, and they headed off. Charles booked a suite at the gorgeous Four Seasons Resort Maui @ Wailea, where they receive V.I.P. treatment upon arrival, and Veronica seems pleased. Everything about Maui is breathtakingly beautiful, and she loves being there, so she suggests they stay a little longer, and of course, Charles agrees.

While Veronica is relaxing by the pool in a private cabana, Charles goes over the Colorado Cannabis farm portfolio with all the details of the necessary equipment needed from start to finish. The total for everything they need is roughly one million dollars. When she returns to the suite, he presents it to her and explains the required equipment's cost details. She goes over the steep numbers and hesitates to decide. The farm is in both her and Art's name, so she wants to make sure she will have a leg to stand on after buying all the equipment. Charles reminds her that the market is growing fast, so they need to act on it as soon as possible, and she agreed.

Charles contacted the manufactures to confirm the orders for all the equipment. Realizing he is right, he feels nervous but glad he is taking the initiative to get it going. Her available cashflow is steady from the four Santa Monica condo rentals and the guesthouse rental from her tenant who works in sales.

The first thing on her to-do list when she gets home is to talk with her tenant to see if he will renew his lease or not. Art's properties are paid for, so her expenses are minimal, with her only paying for the essential upkeep like the cleaning and gardening services, utilities, and taxes. She also wants to see if Maria the housekeeper would consider moving into one of the rooms in lieu of a reduced salary. Art paid her around five thousand dollars a month, but she had living expenses by maintaining her own place. By moving in, Veronica would only have to pay her about three thousand dollars a month. Charles can see the more she dives into the realities of what's ahead, the less time she focuses on what is behind her, the loss of their baby girl.

On the flight home from Maui, Veronica gets a call from her guesthouse tenant. He had just returned from Cali for the weekend after having a B.B.Q. with some friends at the house. He slowly and hesitantly told her there was a fire. A fire? Veronica abruptly shouted. He threw the charcoals in the trash in the garage before he left for Cali. Unfortunately, when he returned home, the entire guesthouse had burned down. In shock but trying to remain calm, Veronica feels panicked, so her first question to him was, was it just the guest house that burned? He told her, yes, and Veronica could not believe this happened.

The main house is ok, but the guesthouse and Art's cars were all destroyed. The beautiful Bentley, Mercedes, Range Rover, and her Audi are a thing of the past. Charles drove the pickup truck and always parked it on the backside of the main house's circular driveway, so it was untouched. The guesthouse tenant's rent is gone, so now she needs to speak with Maria about possibly reducing her salary if she agrees to move in. Charles returned to the club to do security and the car dealership to generate money. Veronica needs a car, so he ordered one and is due to arrive soon. The Colorado farm equipment will arrive within the next thirty days, but they can't process anything until it's all installed. In the meantime, Veronica contacted the insurance company to file a claim.

The adjuster contacted Veronica the next day and asks her about Art because the policy shows him as the sole owner named on the deed. Veronica explained to her that Art is deceased and left the house to her, but she just hasn't changed the title yet. The adjuster replied, "Yes, we know Mr.

Graziani is deceased, and you and Leilani Bourdeaux were the beneficiaries. For this claim of five hundred thousand dollars, I will need a certified copy of his living trust that shows you as the beneficiary of his home". Veronica's heart skipped a beat, so she sat down. Thinking fast, she said, "Oh, I have a copy of the trust, I can give it to you." The adjuster said, "ok, it needs to be a certified filed copy." Ok, Veronica said and ended the call.

Veronica had Arts Attorney rewrite the body of the original version of the trust naming her as the primary beneficiary and attached the front copy of the initial trust just to give to Leilani. The original copy of the living trust has the legal stamp at the bottom of every page, naming Leilani as the primary beneficiary. She knew Leilani would not contest anything because she's just not savvy about legal matters like this. The problem is, the trust she has is fake, drawn up by Art's attorney, who is long gone somewhere in Mexico. Veronica doesn't know what to do, so the next day, she emailed the adjuster and told her she would be out of town for the next couple of weeks, so she would rather hold off on the claim until she returns. She took the loss and paid for it herself to avoid the obvious implications of breaking the law.

She doesn't have a car, and her readily available cash is depleting fast. Part of the insurance company's claim was to have a demolition company clear out and level the guesthouse's space. She also needed the destroyed cars towed to eliminate the eyesore so they can start the rebuild. She and Charles put their heads together, and he told her not to worry; he's back at the club doing security work at night and selling cars during the day so that they'll be just fine. Charles doesn't know the truth about the trust, and now is not the time to tell him, so she says ok and thinks about what to do next.

Meanwhile, her tenant is asking for his deposit of two thousand dollars back so he can move. She ponders on whether to give it to him or not. He was the one who caused the fire in the first place by negligently leaving the charcoal embers in the trashcan and going out of town. Knowing all his belongings were in the guesthouse, she put herself in his position and just gave him the deposit back. Veronica is starting to become overwhelmed again, slowly slipping back down that dark road.

Charles enjoys being back at the club because it is an exciting place to be. Everyone is happy, always in good moods, and the beautiful girls are young and plentiful. One Saturday night, Charles noticed a young lady he had never seen before. She is knock out gorgeous, and he can't take his eyes off her but remains professional and reserved. She returned to the club the following week, and this time, they made eye contact. He winked and slowly licked his lips, showing interest. Shy, she smiled and walked to the dance floor. He watched her throughout the night to see what type of guys approach her and who catches her interest. She's with a girlfriend, so several guys come to them, but they don't seem to be very interested. He notices the guys didn't buy them any drinks, so he sent them two rounds on the house.

The next time Charles saw her was a couple of weeks later, and she is lovely as ever. She looks bi-racial, but he's not sure. Suddenly, a fight broke out; he diffused it, but just as the other security crew started escorting the guys out, the crowd heard gunshots, which caused a panic. Chaos spread throughout the club as everyone desperately tried to exit the building. With all hands on deck, the rest of the security staff immediately direct the crowd towards the rear emergency exit to remove them from harm's way. In the scuffle, he sees her crouching down on the floor with her friend, so he signals to one of the agents that he's going to take care of them. With so much commotion, she cut her hand on a broken piece of glass, so he approaches to render aid and calls 911.

While waiting for the paramedics, Charles chats with her to keep her calm. She is such a fresh and beautiful woman up close; he can hardly contain himself. While saying her name, he wanted to suck the breath right out of her mouth, standing just inches from her face. He quickly explains that someone from the office needs to write an incident report, and she said ok. When the paramedics arrive, they dress her wound and suggest she get a couple of stitches just in case, so her wound will heal nicely. Charles being the gentleman that he is, volunteers, to drive them to the hospital.

Charles and Veronica's relationship and sex life have slowly dwindled to almost nothing lately, leaving him open to exploring other possibilities. Veronica's difficulty was getting over the baby's loss, among other stressors testing his loyalty. Charles and Giselle chat on the way to the hospital, and he finds her not only beautiful but also smart. She recently graduated from college and has only been living in Vegas for less than a year.

They are both attracted to each other, and she likes that protective spirit about him, so she gives him her number. After getting a few stitches, Charles drove them back to the club to get his truck. Being a gentleman and not wanting the night to end, he invited the two ladies for breakfast, and they gladly accepted. They went to an all-night diner off the strip, and as their conversation continued, Charles talked more about himself, and Giselle seems to be intrigued. They eat, Charles pays the bill and leaves a generous tip, and they all walk back out to the car. Again, he volunteers to drive them both home, and he can Uber back to the club, and they said ok, and thank you.

First, he safely drops off her friend and then continues to Giselle's house. They share the same taste in music, and as their conversation gets more profound, she finds him more and more enjoyable. He is an attractive man, muscular, but his intelligence is so refreshing that she is happy to hang out with a guy who seems to be together. He adds her address into the Uber app, and when they arrive at her house, the Uber pulls up about a minute later. They get out of the car, and she reaches up to hug and thank him. As they embrace, his hard-muscular body against hers makes her melt. Damn, she thought, he feels good, and he smells good. He held on to her a little longer than usual, and she did not want him to let her go, but she broke away because she felt a little aroused by his embrace and his cologne. As their faces met, after releasing their embrace, their cheeks connected. Her face felt so good to him, on instinct, he gently kissed her cheek and bid her a good night. His soft lips felt like two pillows on her face, sending a tingle down her spine as well as other places. She walked away, smiling, hoping he will call her soon.

On Monday morning, he had a beautiful exotic flower arrangement delivered to her with an enclosed card saying *Be well gorgeous. I hope to see you again soon, Charlie 702.929.0817"*. Giselle had never seen such a beautiful arrangement in her life. She knew it must've cost at least a few hundred dollars, and she's glad he's not cheap. She thought about how his lips felt on her cheek, and she immediately called to thank him. He is at the car dealership and answers her call. Glad to hear from her, they chat for a minute, then he asks if she would like to meet for lunch on Wednesday. She accepts and says she would love to meet him for lunch. "Great, he said, I will text you the info, and I will see you there at one o'clock." "Ok, great, she said, see you then." Excited, she is looking forward to seeing him again so soon.

Giselle arrives at the restaurant and is seated at a white table clothed table for two. Just as she sits down, Charles walks in, and she looks at him, thinking he's better looking than she remembered. He looked so freaking fresh, and he had on a different cologne but smelled just as impressive as he did the night they met. When they met, most of their time was at night, and now in the daylight, Charles is better looking than she thought. He looks like a young Rock with a Denzel swag. His skin is smooth, and he has great teeth, which is crucial to her. She didn't see what she had a taste for on the menu but noticed they had all the items she wanted. She felt like having a seafood crepe, with scallops, shrimp, and crabmeat with a light cream sauce. The server suggested that the Chef come out to describe to him directly what she wanted to have. Wow, she thought, how cool is that? The Chef came out, and politely introduced himself to them, and she described the dish, and he made it exactly how she wanted it.

What a delightful afternoon they shared, and she can't wait to see Charles again. She likes him, and he is attracted to her, but he is trying to keep it casual because he feels guilty about Veronica. He plays it cool, so instead of inviting her out to dinner, he tells her the club is celebrating its tenth anniversary on Saturday, and they have a private event that is invitation only. He would like to add her and her girlfriend to the guest list. She accepted and is looking forward to it.

All the equipment arrived at the farm in Colorado, so the installations can now begin. Veronica is not working, so to save money, she booked a commercial flight to Colorado because it's cheaper than fueling the jet and paying a pilot. She wants to oversee everything coming together because she spent a lot of money to get this business going. She'll be gone at least a week or two and reminded Charles about the demolition company coming to get rid of the burnt cars and the remaining rubble from the guesthouse. She put the claim on hold because of the issues about the Living Trust. In the meantime, she considers making a claim about her car in the fire. She knows all of Art's expensive luxury cars are a loss, and she cringes with anger and disappointment, just thinking about it.

Saturday night is the anniversary celebration at the club, so Charles is excited. The club spared no expense with the food, décor, or the booze. The gala also serves as a charity event, so each table costs $200 per person, with the proceeds going to local organizations that help special needs kids and women's abuse shelters. The club is packed with at least one thousand guests attending, and Charles paired the two ladies at a table with people who are good to know. Sitting at their table are; an Attorney and his wife, a UNLV professor and her husband, a physician and his wife, the car dealership owner, and his girlfriend.

Giselle is looking stunning, and just the sight of her takes his breath away. She is wearing a fitted sequenced, mermaid style dress, and the color compliments her skin tone perfectly. Her radiant aura commands everyone's attention at the table, and Charles is proud she is his invite. They enjoy great conversations, lots of drinking, eating great food, and Charles snuck in a few slow dances with her. It's a great night, and Giselle is having a great time. His body feels so good with hers, and she is starting to feel more relaxed with him.

The two of them are having such a good time together, and for a moment, he forgets about Veronica. He hasn't felt this happy in quite some time and wants to hold on to it and her forever. Veronica represents so much grief and despair in his life, and they barely manage to coexist lately. From losing the baby and the fire's losses, he forgot how to smile, have fun, and be happy. To him, Giselle is a nice distraction; she is so full of life, so sexy and beautiful. More importantly, she is a delight to be around, which makes him feel alive again. With no sorrow and no worries, just the sound of her laughter is a breath of fresh air to him. Veronica will be out of town for at least two weeks. He is falling for Giselle fast and wants to make love to her tonight, but he's committed to Veronica. Although his desire for Giselle is strong, he wants to be sincere, so he holds back.

For now, he gives her a long but soft peck on her lips. His lips are so thick and smooth; she reciprocates with a lavish opened mouth, passionate kiss. The progression of their kiss arouses them both, and they knew they had to have each other. Again, he resists and breaks their embrace. It's late, the party is over, and he thanks her for coming and ends the evening by telling her he will see her again soon. The next day he calls and invites her to dinner.

Charles made dinner reservations for the two of them. He picked her up at five o'clock and drove over by the airport. He pulled into Maverick Helicopters to take the twilight flight over the strip. Looking at all the lights of the strip was fun, and she loved it. Next, they headed north to the Strat at Top of the World, the highest restaurant in Vegas. It's the only rotating, high rise restaurant that overlooks the entire valley. The night was very romantic, and the two of them are getting closer. So many things are going through his mind right now, he feels torn. He doesn't know whether he should have an affair or just break up with Veronica. They've been together a long time, and he even asked her to marry him, but it all got put on hold after the baby died. He feels empty when he's with Veronica, but he's happy and feels alive with Giselle. More importantly, he sees his future.

He doesn't want to let her go, but he also knows he can't just keep her in limbo. He backs off a bit to see what she does. After dinner, he took her home and ended the night with a kiss.

Charles called Giselle two days later to say hi and find out how she was doing. He purposely kept the conversation casual, trying to see where her head was. Knowing she's single but as beautiful as she is, it won't be for long. He needs to do something before that happens. Giselle was hoping he would ask her out again, but he didn't. Veronica is to return home from Colorado soon, so he didn't want to risk anything. She called him with updates on everything, and her spirits seemed to be up as there was a slight amount of excitement in her voice. She texted him pictures to show all the progress, and he complimented her on a job well done. At the end of their conversation, she mentioned that she needed to stay another week, and he said ok. Just the thing he needed to hear; now he can focus back on Giselle. He wants to continue seeing her, so he booked a private cabana at Costa di Mare at the Wynn for a delicious Mediterranean/Italian dinner. It's one of the most romantic restaurants to dine in Vegas, and Giselle couldn't be more delighted.

Veronica's car gets delivered the day before she returns home. He ordered a fully loaded Titanium Metallic Model S Tesla with a white interior. He already installed the High-Power wall connector on the house's side since they no longer have a garage. He took it for a short test drive and is confident she will love it. He got everything all cleared out from the fire and hired a contractor to start rebuilding a six-car garage where the guesthouse used to be. The building will be large enough for all the cars once they are replaced and won't have to be parked right next to each other. Veronica called, saying she will be home on Thursday, and she gave him the flight number and the time she lands.

Charles pulls into the passenger pickup area at McCarran; he sees Veronica sitting on the bench, looking at the approaching cars. Not noticing him pulling up, he lets the window down and says, "Hey, Miss lady." Veronica looked over at him and is in shock to see what he's driving. She smiled, quickly walked over to the car, immediately jumped in, and kissed him on the cheek. He's fresh and clean, just the way she likes. They've been apart for a few weeks, and she misses him. Sitting in that brand-new car made her feel alive again. He quickly hopped out to grab her luggage and placed it in the trunk. When he got back in, seeing the look on her face told him everything he needed to know. He made the right choice; she loves the car. Smiling, with a sense of accomplishment, he drove the long way home. He asks if she's hungry, and she said yes. He turned the volume on high to H.E.R. station on Pandora and headed west to Summerlin to enjoyed their favorite Thai dishes at Nittaya's Secret kitchen.

Chapter Three

Vegas meets LA

Leilani is finally getting the hang of being a mom and having Tony and Giselle with her makes everything easier. It's the end of summer, and Arabella Love is now six months old and meeting all her milestones quite nicely. She is a happy, healthy baby, full of giggles, laughs, and smiles, and Leilani's heart is whole. Thinking about the upcoming holiday, Leilani decided to take a trip out to Cali since her cousins have never been there. She needs to check on Santa Monica B.S.G. so that they can kill two birds with one stone. When she mentioned it to them, they were excited and can't wait. So, it's a road trip to Cali, and Leilani rented a large S.U.V. to have plenty of space for all their stuff with Tony at the wheel.

When they arrived in L.A., just minutes away from Santa Monica, Tony and Giselle enjoy the scenery and are looking forward to what they've always heard about the L.A. scene. Almost at the restaurant, Leilani points out the complex of the four Condos that Art owned, mentioning they were all given to Veronica, which Giselle thought was strange. Leilani had forgotten about those Condos until just now driving by them. Giselle didn't want to seem nosey and pry, but she did not understand why Leilani only received insurance money when she was carrying his child. Leilani explained to her that Art died before either of them even knew about her pregnancy. Even though they were close, Leilani figured he had his reasons for leaving everything to Veronica, plus she was so distraught, she wasn't even thinking straight at the time. She was too busy, grieving.

They arrive at the restaurant about an hour before opening, and Tony looks around and loves it. "Wow, cousin, I love this place; I could see myself working here! You have that beautiful ocean view and state of the art kitchen. How is this place doing?" Leilani replied, "It's doing very well, which is why I don't have to be here all the time. You are welcome to work here if you like; it's up to you." Tony smiled and said, "My job in Vegas is cool, but I will keep this place in mind. What about you, Giselle?" "No, I think I'll stay in Vegas for a while; I kind of like it there. It's small and not so hectic, and besides, I like helping Leilani with the baby". "Thank you, cousin, so let me give you the grand tour." As the staff prepares the main dining room for opening, they all graciously greet Leilani and congratulate her on the baby.

Everyone gathers around to see the baby saying how cute she is and looking just like Art. While the staff is admiring Arabella, the manager pulls Leilani to the side and tells her what's going on. He told Leilani that everyone's condo rent has practically doubled. As much as they all appreciate the opportunity to live there so close to work, with the original amount being way less than the average surrounding rental properties, they are all having difficulty paying the increased amount. He also mentioned that he realized the discounted rent was supposed to be suitable for at least one year, but they had no idea the rent would increase so much after one year. Leilani asked what the rent was? When they all first arrived, he told her that the rent was only one thousand dollars a month because they agreed to relocate, and the low rent allowed them to adapt themselves to Cali. Still, last month, their rent increased to twenty-five hundred dollars, which is the area's going rate.

Leilani had no idea that Veronica raised the rent on the condos', but she explained that Art owned the condos, and unfortunately, when he passed, Veronica inherited them. She also explained that she has not been in touch with Veronica since Arts death over a year ago last May but will see what she can do to help. Learning this bothered her, and as much as she never wants to see Veronica again, she feels compelled to reach out to her to see if there is anything she can do. Just around the corner, a few steps away, Giselle and Tony were standing with Arabella while the staff took turns holding her, and Giselle overheard their conversation and kept a mental note of it.

Leilani booked three adjoining rooms at a charming boutique hotel not far from the restaurant, and after unpacking and freshening up, they explore the city for the afternoon. First, they walked across the street to the famous Santa Monica pier and took lots of pictures. After walking along the pier for a while, they work up an appetite, so they went back to the restaurant to eat. Tony was impressed and enjoyed the whole dining experience, but especially the taste of everything. After eating, they drove to Hollywood to see the Grauman's Chinese Theater and walked along the legendary Walk of Fame. After shopping and taking pictures, they drove up to Hollywood Hills along the winding streets to look at the rich and famous beautiful custom homes. Tony and Giselle are taking it all in, and Leilani can see their enthusiasm. Arabella is also enjoying all the sightseeing and not being fussy.

The following morning, after having a delicious breakfast at Blue Daisy Café on Broadway, they drove to Beverly Hills to tour the Historic Edward L. Doheny, Greystone Estate. The tour takes about three hours but worth every second. It's such a beautiful property, and it took their breath away. After the tour, they went to Rodeo Drive to window shop, and then they drove south down La Cienega to View Park, Ladera Heights, Leimert Park, Baldwin, and Windsor Hills areas to take in the rich Black culture and ate lunch at Simply Wholesome. By the time they arrived back at the hotel in Santa Monica, they were exhausted but very happy about everything they experienced. The next day after breakfast at Jinky's Cafe, Leilani took them to Venice to give them a different perspective of the southern California beach coastline. She explained other beaches within L.A. county are in several neighboring cities, including Santa Monica, Malibu, Redondo, Hermosa, Playa Del Rey, and Long Beach, to name a few. Walking along Venice beach was an experience of its own. Full of shopping, food, and unique people to watch, they loved it, and Tony and Giselle didn't realize how culturally diverse and unique L.A. was. It has been a great three days for all of them, and they take home some beautiful memories and great pictures. It was a fantastic three-day mini-vacation, and on Monday morning, they returned to Vegas, back to the grind.

As Tony drives, the ladies ride in the back to talk and play with Arabella. Giselle points out how much she looks like Art from all the pictures that she has seen of him, so she starts to ask more questions. Leilani acknowledges her comment and agrees. Leilani tells her about him and reminisces on how the two of them met. She explained to Giselle Art was a very wealthy man, which she discovered over time, and that he was a kind, caring, and loving person. She went on to say that she considered him to be her best friend, and he was a vital part of the best ten years of her life. She told her about the original B.S.G. in Vegas and how it burned down. She also told her about the private jet, the condos in Santa Monica, and the vacation home in the Hamptons. Giselle tried not to show her surprise hearing all that Leilani was telling her, and couldn't understand how Art had so much and left it to his assistant. Leilani talked about their travels worldwide and how people who were closest to them thought they were a couple over the years. She also told her the backstories about Veronica and Philippe and the last trip they all took together for Art's birthday just before he passed away.

Oh, Giselle asked, so his assistant Veronica was also one of the beneficiaries? Yes, since his parents were deceased and his only son Philippe died in the crash with him, he had no other family, so she and I were the only beneficiaries of his estate. As Leilani continued to divulge more about Art, she realized they lived a great life together, and never in her wildest dreams did she ever think she would do all those things so early in life. She hates talking about it because it almost feels like she is reliving the pain of losing him all over again, but at the same time, it feels therapeutic to open up about it and not keep her feelings buried inside.

By the time they returned to Vegas, Giselle had a much clearer picture of Art and feels sad that Leilani is raising little Arabella alone without him. But, after hearing the details, she wants to dig a little deeper. Leilani gets on her computer to reset the payroll salaries for her management staff at B.S.G., who stay at the condos. She gives each of them a monthly increase of one thousand dollars to help cover their housing costs because right now, she does not want to deal with Veronica.

August is the hottest month of the summer in Vegas. With September approaching, the weather starts to cool down as October prepares for the winter season. On Halloween, the weather turns from hot to cold like the flip of a switch. Giselle loves giving kids Halloween candy and lucky for Leilani's neighborhood kids because they get the regular-sized candy bars. She and Leilani help the staff at the Mothers Nest decorate the center, and those kids also get lots of candy.

The months Giselle has been in Vegas, she has been working for a temp agency. Leilani has an open position available for a Program Director at the center, with a starting annual salary of fifty-thousand-dollars, so she offered it to Giselle, which she gladly accepted. Giselle likes the center's concept, offering struggling mothers the opportunity to get their lives together while raising their children in a peaceful and enriching environment.

As Thanksgiving rolls around, it'll be the second one at the house for Leilani and Tony, but it's the first one for baby Arabella and Giselle. They plan a big feast of all the traditional holiday foods, and everyone chips in to prepare what they make best. This year the menu consists of herb-roasted turkey, Peking duck, a honey glazed ham, a prime rib roast, cornbread dressing with gravy, collard greens, green beans, mac and cheese, candied yams, home-made cranberry sauce, and several desserts like peach cobbler, cakes, and pies. They made enough to feed an army, so Leilani always makes tv dinners and freezes them to eat later.

After dinner, Leilani went into her office to check on the Kids Christmas files. Her Program Director usually starts on this task to ensure they have everything they need in time for Christmas. The center makes most of the purchases online because of the convenience, and Giselle offers to help. "Great Leilani explains, this will be a part of your job as the new Program Director. Normally you would do this in the office, but I brought the files home since she doesn't work for me anymore. Every file should have a cover page on the left with their names, ages, and sizes with subfiles showing everything they received the previous year. Once we purchase everything, we take pictures so we can make good choices the following year. You will see they get; a pair of shoes, three toys, a coat, and a bike, but some of them got a bike last year and won't need another one this year, so for those kids, purchase everything except the bikes. Some of the older kids don't even want toys; they'd rather have all clothes and shoes. That's why we keep the files, so keep that in mind. Just make sure you pick out something different from what they got last year; I'm very picky about that".

"We have forty kids this year, and the total budget is twenty thousand dollars. I like to spend five hundred on each kid, so you can pick out whatever you want; just make sure to stay within that budget. I'm sure they will love whatever you choose, but please be creative. You will find that the older teenaged kids make a wish list, making it easier for you. My corporate sponsors pay for the kids' presents, and I buy each mom a five-hundred-dollar gift card. We have twenty moms, so I spend ten thousand myself. Here is the credit card to pay for everything, and make sure once you complete the orders for each kids' file, put a yellow tab on it. Take pictures of every item that arrives. Check off the forms showing the items received and mark it as complete by adding a checkmark next to each itemized gift. Once everything is received, put a green tab on the folder and put it back in the box to be filed away at the office. That way, we know which files are complete. I know this seems like a lot, but you have a whole month to do it."

"When making your selections, think of these kids as being yours. You don't want to buy ten of the same dolls or twenty of the same shoes. Make sure you pick out unique gifts for each child and make sure they are age-appropriate. When those kids open their presents in front of the tree on Christmas day, they will be excited. They need to know the gifts are especially for them and not random. That's why we take pictures and keep such detailed records. Also, we encourage the moms to look in the files to see what we bought to make sure they don't make duplicate purchases. As the gifts arrive, you check it off on each kids' list, add the pictures to the file and complete it. Usually, the Director has the clerical team gift wrap, label everything, and put the presents under the tree." "Ok, wow, Giselle said, I love this idea." "Yes, Leilani noted, it's a lot of work, but so worth it."

"The center is one of my passions and the one I'm proudest of because, to me, it's all about paying it forward. The name of this event is *December to Remember.* Art was a dedicated philanthropist and watching him over the years be as giving as he was, warmed my heart. He helped me get this institution started, and I will be forever grateful to him. You would be surprised how many companies come on board donating hundreds of thousands of dollars to help an organization like this, and that's a big deal to me. We have a year-round job training program to support, assist, and train our residents to obtain and keep jobs, including computer training classes. And for the moms who struggle to meet the qualifications of conventional employment, we offer them an opportunity to work at the center. Some residents will work in the kitchen or with the cleaning crew. Some drive the shuttle buses or work in the office with the clerical team. We have three teens working in the office now."

"The Christmas season is very busy at the center, but my favorite time of year is spring, of course." "Why is spring your favorite time of year?" Leilani smiled and said, "Because it's right after the chilling winter and just before the summer's blazing heat. Spring is the time when everything blooms like the cherry blossoms, the roses, the gazanias, the grass is at its greenest, and the weather is just perfect." Giselle grabbed the box of files already coded yellow to complete the process. She then went on the computer to all the online websites to see the carts that are ready to be checked out, so she just needs to make the payments.

Giselle was relieved. All she had to do was check each gift off as they arrive, take the pictures, mark the files as complete, and have the presents wrapped. The previous Program Director had a perfect system of keeping track of everything. She noticed she started shopping back in October, and it was just like Leilani explained it. Inside the files were pictures of each child along with their report cards. She went through each file and could see that most of the kids grew up at the center, and she smiled.

Later that night, Giselle is in the mood to get out and dance, so she and her girlfriend go to the club, and she's hoping to see Charles. He is there, it's been a while, and they're both happy to see each other. Charles watches her walk through the club, and she is looking lovelier than ever. He feels torn because he is still technically with Veronica. As Giselle walks towards Charles, they smile and hug each other tightly. Her perfume and body so close to his are intoxicating, and she is also mesmerized by his. They chat and make small talk, catching up, and he offers them a drink. As soon as he walks over to the bar to get the drinks, two guys approach the two ladies like hungry wolves. Charles turns around and sees the two guys and has the server take the drinks over to them and disappears to the other side of the club. He instead sends her a text saying, *I miss you,* with heart emojis.

As the two guys try their best lines, Giselle, uninterested, looks down at her phone and sees Charles' message and smiles. He misses her and wants to see her in private. One of the guys tries to get her attention by asking her to dance, and she agrees. They walk over to the dance floor as Charles watches. As Giselle feels the music's rhythm and gets into her groove, she glances over and spots Charles and looks at him the entire time of her dance. She is moving in such provocative and sensual ways; he can't take his eyes off her. They lock eyes and silently convey their attraction for each other as if no one else is in the club. The music is intensely loud, and the dark rooms colorful lights are flickering like a kaleidoscope as the alcohol guides her moves. She continues to dance for the next few songs, then finally takes her seat for a pause, and Charles sends her another text, saying; *meet with me tonight*. Smiling, she replies, ok, and looks up to where he was last standing, but he's not there. She scans the crowded club looking for him, but she doesn't see him.

Charles went upstairs to the office to get on the computer to make a reservation. Afterward, he sends her another text. Meet me at the Café at the Wynn whenever you are ready. Giselle's phone is now in her purse while she parties on the dancefloor, so she doesn't see his text. She dances to a few more songs, and her friend is also having a great time. She grabs her phone, reads his latest message, and responds, "*Ok, I'm ready now. I'll see you there*". She tells her friend she is ready to go but will take an Uber. "Ok, girl, her friend said, I'm having a blast, talk to you later." Giselle orders an Uber, leaves the club and meets Charles at the Wynn. The Café is open twenty-four hours and is an excellent place to dine even in the wee hours of the morning. As she takes a seat, Charles walks in from behind. He quietly approaches her, softly grabs her shoulders, bends down, and kisses her neck. Delighted, she looks up, and then Charles kisses her lips. She is attracted to this man, but she doesn't understand why he hasn't made any serious moves with her.

They eat, drink, laugh, catch up, and enjoy each other's company for a couple of hours or so. Giselle looks at her watch and says, it's getting late; "I'm getting a little tired. I should probably go.". Not wanting the night to end, Charles suggests she stay because he reserved a room for them. Feeling horny, she accepts his invitation, and they take the elevator upstairs to a corner panoramic king suite on the twenty-eighth floor. The room is elegant and spacious, almost seven hundred square feet with joining floor to ceiling windows, with the curtains fully drawn to capture the full view of the strip. On every table of the room are flowers as well as in the bathroom. As she takes in all the luxury of this room, she spots chocolates on the bed and a bottle of good wine right next to it, and she smiles. She is reminded of their date from Top of the World that night they took the strip's helicopter ride.

Charles wraps his big strong arms around her waist and cups her perky breasts, and her arousal heightens to level seven. As she turns to face him, they passionately kiss like they haven't seen each other in ages. He leads her into the bathroom, and they both disrobe and step into the shower. While kissing, they generously lather each other with a fragrant body wash from head to toe. The warm water glides down and washes away the lathered soap while they continue to kiss and explore each other's bodies. When they step out of the shower, he wraps her in a soft white terry cloth robe, picks her up, and walks over to the bed. He gently lays her down, opens the robe revealing her hot naked body that's ready and willing to receive him. He grabs her foot and works his way up to her inner thigh to devour her like a cupcake. Masterfully skilled, he gently sucks and manipulates her pearl, achieving a full erection with his lips and tongue, as her arousal pulsates to level ten. She grabs his hands and arches her back, enjoying all the pleasure he is giving her. He carefully watches her movements and listens as her breaths begin to slow down and become quiet. Suddenly, she bursts into a full aquatic climax, and he takes it all in.

This night feels right, and he wants to make love to her, but hesitates and lies beside her. His body is so big and robust; she can't help but turn over to go down on him. As she puts his huge semi-erect penis into her mouth, she is shocked when he becomes fully erect. He is much bigger than she expected, and she can't wait to have him inside of her. She continues to lick and suck him until he can't take it anymore, so he pulls her up, so they are face to face and enters her, thrusting in and out over and over, tapping her G spot, sending her into another orgasmic ocean of pleasure. He then flips over and pumps her doggy style, squeezing and slapping her plump ass with one hand while grabbing her long ponytail with the other hand, making him explode. Catching their breath, they fall on their backs, on to the pillows, and drift off to sleep. Just a few hours later, as the sun rises, it lights up the entire suite. They sheepishly wake up in each other's arms, and he whispers in her ear. "I like you," and she smiles. They shower, leave the suite, and he takes her home. He kisses her one more time, bids her a good day, and says he will see her soon.

Arriving home, he walks into the bedroom and finds Veronica still sleeping, so he goes back downstairs to begin his daily exercise routine in their gym. The gym has all the equipment that keeps his body in optimal shape, so he is grateful to enjoy a private work out. After his workout, Veronica wakes up, goes to the kitchen, puts on a pot of coffee, grabs a yogurt, and gets on the office's computer. As Charles walks towards the office, she hears his footsteps and greets him with the same level of unenthusiastic hello that she's given him for the past few months, and in turn, he says good morning. He stands on the threshold of the door to see if she will look up from the computer, but she doesn't. The flame of their relationship has diminished to a spark, and Charles is seriously contemplating ending it. They have been through many things over the eight years, and the plans of marriage have unfortunately taken a back seat.

Without looking up at him, Veronica told him only the garage would be rebuilt and not the guesthouse because they must pay for it themselves, and he asks why. She made up a lie and said she neglected to pay the bill, so the insurance company is unwilling to pay out on such a high claim from a lapsed policy. He mentioned it would cost thousands of dollars to rebuild the garage, and since they won't get the rental money from the tenant anymore, he asks what's her plan for the money. She never took her eyes off the computer. She said not to worry because she raised all the rent on the four condos in Santa Monica. The money coming in from the

Hamptons Air B & B rental is more than enough to cover their expenses instead of worrying about the guesthouse's loss of rent. He glared at her, shakes his head, says ok, and finally, she looked up at him as he turned and walked away. She wants to sell the house and move, but it's still in Art's name, so it won't happen anytime soon.

Giselle began to think about all the things Leilani told her about Art, and it bothers her that he gave everything he owned to his assistant Veronica. She went into the office to look through Leilani's files to see if she could find some answers. She looks through the file cabinets, and right away, she found a folder that says Art's Estate. There were two sealed manilla envelopes inside the file. The first envelope she opened was a copy of the trust that said everything Leilani told her with everything going to Veronica. Okay, she thought, but then she opened the second envelope and was shocked by what she read. It was the same trust, with all the exact wording, but it shows Leilani as the primary beneficiary, not Veronica.

As she continues reading, she compares every word in each document and could not believe her eyes. First, there are many more assets disclosed in the trust that Leilani didn't mention. The itemized assets were dozens of stocks, bonds, and shareholdings of several fortune 500 companies, plus two bank accounts with ninety million-dollar balances. Immediately her heart began to race, and she frantically turned back to the cover pages of both documents over and over, trying to see the differences. Shaking her head, she grabbed both files and ran up to her room to study them privately. Once in her room, she carefully read each document and finally figured it out. One copy was certified with initials on every page on the bottom right corner, and the other one wasn't. Seeing the differences with both envelopes sealed made her wonder if Leilani was even aware of it. The wheels are now turning in Giselle's head, and she is determined to get to the bottom of it.

Giselle is thinking about how to best approach Leilani with her findings. Her cell phone rang, and it's Charles. Her response to him is a little curt, so he asked if she is ok. She takes a deep breath and tells him she will talk to him about it later and ends the call. A few minutes later, he sent her a text saying, "*let's meet for lunch tomorrow at twelve,*" and she replied, ok. Giselle knows that Leilani was content with receiving the one hundred thousand dollars and the four million from his life insurance. Still, after looking at these documents, she knows they should have a conversation. Giselle recalled when Leilani came out to New Orleans when they all went out, and Leilani talked with the Priestess. She remembered the Priestess told her about losing something of great value, and Giselle thinks this must be what she meant.

The next day, Charles waited for Giselle at the restaurant for lunch, but she forgot and didn't show. Annoyed, he called to ask what happened. She apologized and explained she's having a hectic day at work and asks to take a rain check. He told her, ok, no worries, how about dinner on Friday night. She said yes, and to pick her up from work when she gets off at five. Over the week, Giselle took the time to go over the trust docs and think about approaching Leilani with what she discovered. She wants to talk with

Charles about it to see what he thinks. He picked her up for Friday night's dinner, and they enjoyed a nice dinner at Lola's in Summerlin. As they continued to chat over the dessert, she told him she's been having a challenging situation with her cousin. Charles, not knowing who her cousin is, urges her to go on. She explains to him that her cousin had a baby with a wealthy man who died, but he left just about everything he owned to someone else. Intrigued, Charles asked if the man was married, or was the woman a side chick or something? "No, not at all, Giselle replied; she wasn't a side chick."

Trying not to disclose too many details, Giselle started naming the assets in the trust. He was looking down at his plate eating, and as she began to say them, it sounded familiar, so he stopped eating, looked up at Giselle, and urged her to go on. She described how the guy had a private jet, a mansion here in Vegas, another one in the Hamptons, several cars, some condos in Santa Monica, then suddenly, Charles choked. Giselle asks if he is ok, and he told her yes and to continue. She named everything Art had but didn't say anything about the cannabis farm. Then he asks, "So you say the guy died, was he an older guy"? "No, not that old, maybe about forty-five or fifty, but he died in a plane crash with his son." In shock, Charles tried very hard not to let his feelings show as he slowly leaned forward, continuing to listen with his fullest attention.

Charles asked Giselle, "So you said your cousin had a baby with him, but you said his son died in the crash with him, right?" "No, Giselle said; my cousin had her baby after he died. Her baby was born just this past

February fourteenth, and he died last May. She didn't even know she was even pregnant when he died; she found out weeks later. The son that was with him on the plane was his adult son." She went on to explain that her cousin had known this man for over ten years, and he only left her like a hundred thousand dollars but left everything else to his assistant. Knowing that didn't seem right, she did a little digging and found the proof.

Now Charles' eyes widen with curiosity, and ask her, what proof? Giselle explained her cousin has two different versions of his living trust documents, and they don't match. Giselle figured the assistant must have done some crooked, foul shit with the papers, and she plans to get to the bottom of it. Wow, Charles said. To make sure his thoughts were right, he asked what the guy's name was, and she said, "His name is Art Graziani." Boom, he knew it! Charles often wondered why Art left so much to Veronica, but he had no idea what Leilani got. Even after all the extravagant things he and Veronica did since Art's passing, he never questioned her about it. He didn't know every detail, but he also didn't know what he left for Leilani. Either way, it always seemed strange that Art left so much to Veronica.

Chapter Four

Love is Still a flower that Blooms

When Charles arrived home, Veronica was in the bedroom, crying. Attempting to comfort her, he asked what was wrong. She told him she went to the doctor and was diagnosed with stage four breast cancer, so she needs to have a double mastectomy. He held her in his arms and tried to comfort her for what seemed like hours as she soaks his shirt with tears, so he saves the conversation about Art for later. They haven't been intimate in months, and now he knows why. He draws her a soothing aromatic bubble bath to calm her nerves. Even though their relationship hasn't been at its best lately, he is still a kind and caring person, and he doesn't want to see her hurt in any way. Trying her best to compose herself, she climbs into the tub as he turns on soft music to soothe her nerves.

Two weeks later, Charles took Veronica to the hospital for a double mastectomy. Although still in shock, Charles listened as the Doctors explain the details of her aftercare. Charles visits her daily and reaches out to Giselle at night to get his mind off the depressive reality. He's had time to think about everything Giselle told him, but now is not the time to confront Veronica about it. Deciding to wait, he helped get her through the arduous recovery and back on her feet.

At the time, Charles didn't think twice about why Leilani went back home while they went on a vacation. He thought they were close and had no idea Veronica could be cruel enough to kick Leilani out of Art's house as she did, but he had no say in that. He didn't think about it because, at the time, he thought Art only left her the house and the jet, and he believed the cannabis farm was a joint investment between the two of them. It wasn't until several months later that Charles found out about the condos, the cars, and the Hampton house. Now feeling anxious, he wants to talk with Veronica about it.

A few weeks later, now that she seems to be feeling better and closer to normal despite what she lost, Charles thinks it's the time to bring up what has been on his mind for weeks, so he starts asking her detailed questions. First, he asks about the jet, suggesting that it would be a good idea to sell it so the hospital bill would not take up the bulk of their money. Angerly, she blows him off and says no, she will figure out another way. Then he suggests maybe they should sell the house and move to a smaller one since it's just the two of them, and again she said no. Lastly, he suggests maybe she should consider leasing half of the Colorado land out to someone else who wants to start a cannabis farm of their own. Veronica says, out of frustration, "Now that is something I may consider because that's the only thing that has my name on it." Charles replied, what? Trying not to appear to be in shock, he said, "What do you mean by that? I thought Art legitimately left everything to you". Caught off guard, Veronica said, "Well, he did, it's just very complicated, that's all." At that point,

Charles knew she was lying, and he couldn't have been more disappointed, but instead of arguing, he went to the gym to work out.

After his workout, he reached out to Giselle to invite her to dinner, and she accepted. He took her out to Lake Las Vegas, and they enjoyed a nice dinner and a great conversation at Mimi and Coco Bistro, a lovely French restaurant in the Monte Lago Village right on the lake. He asks how her cousin is doing, which prompts her to show him a picture of Leilani's baby. "Wow, she's a beautiful little girl, he said. So, this is your cousins' baby, the one she had with the rich guy that was born on February fourteenth, right?" "Yes, Giselle said she looks just like her dad, and you have an excellent memory, Sir." Under his breath, Charles said, *yeah, I see that.* Not hearing what he said, Giselle asked him to repeat it. He cleared his throat and just said, yeah, "I bet."

Giselle asked Charles if he ever thought about having kids, or does he want kids? He looked down for a few seconds, then looked up at her and said, "I had a daughter, but she died when she was just six weeks old." "Ooooh, I'm so sorry, babe, what happened"? "She died of crib death; you know SIDS." "Yes, I know what that is; I'm so sorry." "Yeah, that was probably the worse day of my life." "What was her name?" "Alayna Chermaine." Wide-eyed, Giselle said, "Her middle name was Chermaine, not Charmaine?" "Yes, Chermaine, with an (e not an a)," he said. "Oh, wow, I have a cousin named Chermaine."

Hmmm, Charles said, "So hey, what about you? Do you want kids?" "Oh yes, I come from a big family, and we have lots of kids; the bigger the family, the better." "Well, you're so beautiful, and you're smart; any guy would be lucky to have a family with you." She tilts her head to the side and asks, "do you feel lucky?" Blushing, he leaned over to kiss her lips and said, "Yes, I do feel lucky," and they both smile. She is attracted to Charles and can see herself having lots of babies with him.

Giselle's face is so beautiful, and the moonlight shining on her face is intoxicating to Charles. He suggests they get a room at the hotel to wake up with each other on Christmas Day, and she said ok. He excuses himself from the table and says he will be right back. Charles went to the front desk, got them a room, then went out to his truck to grab a two-foot miniature tree with decorations on it and a big duffle bag of gifts looking like Santa Claus. He tipped the hotel's housekeeping staff manager $100 to set up the little tree, place the gifts all around it, and went back to retrieve Giselle. They got on the empty elevator, and he pressed the button for the top floor. They were kissing and groping each other until they arrived at the top. As the elevator door opened, an older couple cleared their throats wanting to get in, which startled them. Embarrassed, they quickly broke their sensual embrace, smiled, and trotted off to their room, laughing from embarrassment like two school kids.

When Charles opened the door, Giselle was pleasantly surprised to see that cute little decorated tree with gifts all around it. She immediately reached up to hug him around his neck, kissing him profusely. Thrilled with joy, he knew he did the right thing. "Oh, my goodness, I want to open these gifts right now," Giselle said. "Well, come on, let's do this!" Like a kid in a candy store, she began to open each gift carefully but full of excitement. Charles gazes at her, merely looking at her slim but toned arms opening the gifts arouses him. As she flexes her arms, pulling on the shiny ribbons, her shoulders and biceps softly glisten. Giselle started with the envelope. Inside is a plane ticket to the Caribbean booked for late summer, and she gasped with eyes wide as saucers because she's never been there. The next gift was in a small rectangular box, and inside was a beautiful Pandora charm bracelet, and he put it on her wrist. The next box, just a little bigger, was black leather gloves that fit perfectly. The fourth gift box, much larger, was a Louis Vuitton purse with a matching wallet inside. Giselle felt like a Queen, and she is overwhelmed with happiness, thinking of how thoughtful he is. She kissed him holding his face with both hands, and said, "I think I'll keep you for a while." Laughing, he said, "Well, I hope so, at least until we take this trip!"

She is so beautiful with happiness glowing all over her face; he wants to make love to her right now. As they passionately kiss, they both tare off each other's clothes and head for the shower. This time, after cleaning their bodies with the warm soapy water splashing on both, she slowly caresses his penis with her hands and mouth, going up and down as he quickly becomes erect. She sucks harder until he is about to explode, but he stops her for now. They run to the bed, and he flips her over to devour her like a wedding cake and eats her slowly, pressing his lips and tongue on her, sucking her pearl while inserting his finger inside, reaching her G-spot until her sweet nectar squirts like a water fountain. Feeling weak but still wanting to feel him inside her, she turns over as he thrusts his big hard penis in her from the back. Fast and hard strokes are paired with long, slow sensual ones until he explodes. They are both drenched with sweat and collapse in each other's arms to catch their breaths, and minutes later, they fall asleep for about an hour, then wake up and do it all over again.

They have incredible chemistry together, and Giselle wonders if they are a couple now or what? Over the months they've been together, she has only been intimate with him, so she feels their relationship is on a deeper level. Feeling his hesitation to acknowledge what they are to each other, she chooses to stay quiet and waits until he brings it up. The next morning when Charles wakes up at sunrise, he gently kisses her on the forehead. Knowing she's tired, he lets her peacefully sleep and quietly leaves. An hour or so later, when she woke up alone, she is puzzled. She reached over to her cell phone to see what time it was and sees a text message from Charles saying, *Merry Christmas babe, I'll call you later. Have a good day.* She gets dressed, gathers her gifts, leaves the tree, orders an Uber, and goes home. When she arrives at Leilani's house, it's still early, and the house is quiet, so she sneaks upstairs to her room and takes a shower to start her day.

Moments later, Leilani wakes up and goes downstairs to start cooking breakfast, and soon after, Tony joins to help her. Arabella is still sleeping, so she tries to get everything done before she wakes up. She tells Tony she got a buyer for BSG. Surprised, he responded, "What? I didn't know it was for sale". "Yeah, now that I have Arabella, it's just too hectic to travel back and forth. I'd like to instead concentrate more on the Mother's

Nest". "Ok, I get it; what did they offer you?" "With everything as is, including the recipes, they offered me $1.3 million. I'm thinking about carrying the loan to pay me monthly over twenty years, which is easier instead of them having to get a conventional loan through the bank." "Ok, that's the ticket right there." "I just want to make sure they keep some of the staff, and they said they would."

Giselle joins them in the kitchen, holding Arabella in her arms, wearing her new twelve charm Pandora bracelet, which Leilani immediately notices. "Ooooh, that is such a lovely bracelet, Giselle. Is that new"? "Yes, this is one of my Christmas gifts." Tony interrupts, asking, "From who"? Giselle smiling ear to ear, replying, "I have a friend who is sweet to me, thank you!" Tony grabs her wrist to get a closer look laughing and says, "Aaaawwwwe shuckie, duckie, that's nice; Sis, who is this guy, and what's his name?" Blushing, she rotates her arm upward to show its sparkle and says, "Yes, it is nice, isn't it?".

"He gave me a Louie bag with a matching wallet too." "A Louis Vuitton bag?" Leilani asked. "Yes, he did, girl, and it's perfect!" "Okay, so it looks like he's got good taste; let me see that bag girl," as Leilani egged her on. Giselle proudly ran upstairs to retrieve the new bag and brought it down to show them. Leilani inspects the purse and reaches inside. She sees the wallet and the airline ticket to the Caribbean. "Hey now, what's this right here cousin, you're taking a trip too?" Smiling, Giselle replies, "Yes, we are, and I can't wait"! They all laugh and walk over to the tree, sipping on hot chocolate and opening gifts. Arabella looks at them and screams with laughter catching them all off guard. They all looked at each other and busted out laughing too. She's so funny and full of energy, with a personality out of this world, and everyone adores her.

Arabella's first Christmas was a big success. They took lots of pictures and enjoyed a delicious holiday dinner. As Giselle and Leilani are cleaning up, Tony is assembling some of the toys for Arabella as she enjoys the festive holiday surrounded by more than she will ever need. Leilani mentions that she wants to start planning Arabella's first birthday celebration, and Giselle is excited to help her plan it. Leilani asks, "Tell me about this guy in your life. Is it serious? From the looks of those gifts, I would say it is". Giselle replies, "Hmmm, it's getting there; he's a great guy, and I'm very attracted to him, but we're taking it slow. How about I invite him to Arabella's birthday party as my special guest, and you can meet him then"? "Ok, that sounds like a plan. I'm looking forward to meeting him," Leilani replied. Tony overheard their conversation and joined in. Tony has been dating a beautiful Puerto Rican/Columbian girl named Isabella. She looks a lot like the Latina singer Shakira, and she has a beautiful three-year-old daughter named Gabriella. She's a sexy firecracker with a thick accent, and he asks if he can invite her. "Of course, you can, Tony, the more, the merrier," Leilani replied.

Veronica has completed the process of the expanders so she can have her breast augmentation. It has been months since she and Charles have been intimate, so she is hoping by having this done, she will feel sexy again, and maybe it can help rekindle their relationship. With so many medical expenses and Charles now knowing the truth, he suggests selling one of the properties, but Veronica still flat out refuses. He wants to allow her to tell the truth, but she remains quiet and always changes the subject. At this point, because she's not honest with him, their conversations turn into arguments, which pushes him away. Them getting married is once again put on hold and about to be a thing of the past.

Arabella's first birthday party is ready to start, and all the guests have arrived to celebrate her. Leilani ordered a small, round six-inch personal cake just for her to demolish. A beautifully custom made two-story gingerbread house just for show, plus a delicious three-tiered red velvet, vanilla, and chocolate sheet cake for everyone to enjoy. She hired a clown, a magician, a videographer, four ponies for the kids to ride, and of course, a bouncy house for the older kids. She also had popcorn and cotton candy machines and three artists to paint the kids' faces.

It's valentine themed, so her big cousin Giselle bought her a beautiful white fancy dress with red hearts all over it. Dozens of arch-shaped red and white balloons and party favors are all over the backyard. The catered food and drinks are served on red and white valentine tablecloths for everyone to enjoy. Tony's girlfriend, Isabella, and her daughter Gabriella came, and she brought her two-year-old niece as well. Tony also invited a few guy coworker friends because it was a party with lots of beautiful single women. Over the year, Leilani made several friends through a Mommy and Me group she belonged to, so she invited them as well. There were about a dozen kids, plus the parents, so it was a friendly, full crowd. As Tony introduced Leilani to his friends, one man captured her attention.

Very good looking, chocolate and tall with a chiseled physique, his friend Hank remarkably resembles the L.A. Clippers Shooting Guard, Lou Williams, but just a shade or two darker, with wavy hair. He speaks with a slight accent, but she's not sure what kind of accent he has. Tony reminded her that his friend would like to bless the guests with his spoken words, and of course, she wants to hear more of him, so she said yes. As the sun was beginning to set, Tony turned the music down to get everyone's attention and introduces his friend Hank to speak. As Hank stands up to speak, Charles walked into the backyard, holding a big gift box for Arabella, and sits next to Giselle as Hank begins to recite the poem.

To Princess Arabella
Today, you are unwrapping gifts, blowing out candles, playing games, eating cake, and having fun.
There are so many things to do, and you are only one.
Happy first birthday!
May you grow up to be smart and wise. I hope you always keep the same innocence in your eyes.
Happy first birthday!
You may be tiny and small, but you have stolen the hearts of one and all.
Happy first birthday!
You are a beautiful sight to see and, in your heart, may happiness always be.
The first of many celebrations as you were born on St. Valentine's day,
I hope and pray, sweet as candy; you will always stay.
Happy first birthday
A year ago, you weren't even here, and now you are a toddler who has no fear.
Arabella Love, it's all about you today so enjoy your special day for another whole year!

Everyone stood up to clap and cheer, and Leilani is touched. She had no idea Tony's friend was planning to do this, so she was so happy the videographer captured the moment. Leilani thanked Hank for coming and especially for the beautiful poem, and instinctively hugged him. She got a little turned on by the smell of his cologne and even more so by his embrace. As they let go of each other, Leilani gingerly walked away to socialize. Everyone is having a good time, and as she walked to each table, she searched for Giselle to chat and meet her new beau. As she walks up to where Giselle is sitting, she is shocked that Charles is sitting with her. He quickly stands up to greet and hug her. Giselle immediately interjects and says, "wait, you two know each other?" Leilani looked at her and said, "Yes, we go way back, but I haven't seen this man in quite a while now. Welcome to my home Charles, how have you been?" Smiling, Charles replied, "I'm doing well, thanks, and I can see you're doing well. Congratulations on having such a beautiful little girl Leilani."

Just then, the party planner asked everyone to please direct their attention over to the gift table. Arabella got lots of gifts, so Giselle and Leilani tag team to help Arabella open them right after each other while the servers pass out slices of cake and gift bags to each guest. The children's gift bags have toys and candies inside. The adult bags have more things like; red ink pens inscribed with Arabella's name, Dove chocolates, Bert's Bees lip balms, travel size hand sanitizers and lotions, and a little photo album capturing Arabella's first twelve months of pictures. Just after sunset, most of the guests start to leave. The remaining few go inside to continue socializing, and Tony's friend Hank stays to join them. The party planner breaks down everything and cleans up, and the kids fell asleep in Arabella's room with the babysitter, so the adults take advantage of the adult time.

Leilani finds Hank to be a great conversationalist and is well informed and opinionated on current issues. He has a refreshing outlook on life, fun to be around, and Leilani is attracted to him. As they nibble on small bite appetizers of cheese, crackers, bruschetta, fruit, and charcuterie, she focuses some of her attention on Charles because she is surprised to see him with her cousin and not Veronica. Tony's girlfriend Isabella is beautiful and quiet, but she participates in the conversations and engages well. As Leilani focuses her attention on her cousin Giselle and Charles, they are taken with each other and appear to be close. Seeing him, she can't help but wonder about Veronica. She thought about asking him about her but decides this is not the best time to bring her up and especially not in front of Giselle. Leilani knew he and Veronica had become a couple and even moved in together at the guesthouse. Considering the circumstances, she decides to save that question to him for another time. For now, she is enjoying these interesting adult conversations, and she is glad to have everyone here with her.

Giselle brings out a word game that allows everyone to get to know each other better, and they all have a blast, cracking up from the hilarious answers everyone gives. They are all having fun, drinking, eating, and laughing, and Leilani noticed it's just after two a.m. Feeling tired, she extends an invitation to stay if they'd like because she doesn't want anyone driving impaired. Of course, everyone accepts her offer and continues the fun, knowing they don't have to go home. After a while, Giselle takes Charles by the hand and leads him up to her bedroom. Leilani sets up her sofa bed for Hank to sleep on, assuring that it's comfortable, and he graciously accepts. Tony and his girlfriend go up to his room, and after thanking Hank again and making sure he has everything he needs, Leilani retires for the night.

After eight that morning, Leilani went down to the kitchen to prepare something for Arabella to eat. She looked over into the family room to get a glimpse of Hank peacefully sleeping on her sofa bed. His smooth, dark, and muscular body under her crisp white Egyptian cotton sheets with all his lusciousness was indeed a sight to see. Looking at his body, she could tell that he works out often. She curiously stares at him longer than she should, wondering what it would be like being with him. It has been quite a while since she's had the pleasure of being with a man, and she can see this handsome hunk of a man lying on her sofa would be addicting.

She tried hard to be as quiet as she could, but she made a noise, and he woke up. And up he was because as he turned his body towards her, she could see the huge bulge of his larger than average penis through the sheet. Wow, she thought, this man is an Adonis. She quickly apologized for waking him up and urged him to go back to sleep. Still, instead, he looked at her with his beautiful and hypnotic eyes. He said, "Oh, good morning, Doll, what time is it?" He apologizes for sleeping in the buff. Fumbling with her words and babbling like a teenager, she nervously blurted out, "no,

69

you're alright, um, I want you to be comfortable, it's ok, really just relax, go back to sleep." She left and went back upstairs, thinking about how Art always called her Doll. An hour later, while Leilani was busy with Arabella, everyone said their goodbyes and headed out. Hank was the last one to leave, and he thanked Leilani for her hospitality and said he hoped to see her again soon. They hugged, he kissed her on the cheek, bid her a good day, and left.

Charles went over to the hospital to check on Veronica. She had the surgery for her new boobs the previous day, so she will be discharged from the hospital and go home if there are no complications. As he walked into the room, Veronica's doctor gives the good news that she can go home, so she is happy. She will have a few weeks of downtime but expects her to recover fully. He took her home and made sure she is comfortable before working out in the gym downstairs.

Bright and early on Monday morning, Giselle is in her office at the Center. A girl from the clerical team walked by her office and noticed a framed collage of photos on her desk. She complimented her on the creativity and looked at the various pictures of her and Charles. Looking closer, she recognized him and said, "Ooooh, I know this guy, his name is Charles, how long have you been with him?" Giselle looked at her and said, "Oh, that's my Boo; how do you know him?" She then said, "hmmm, well, long story short, the girl who got me this job was dating him, and I thought they were practically married or living together. I'm not sure, but anyway, it's been a while since I've seen them, but that's Charlie J for sure". Giselle feeling a little jaded, she asked, "What's the girl's name, the one who got you the job?" "Oh, her name is Veronica," the girl replied. Giselle's heart skipped a beat, and it felt like her heart dropped down to her stomach. Before she let any emotions show on her face, she makes up an excuse to get the girl out of her office immediately by saying she needs to make a call. Shaking and feeling nervous, Giselle reaches for her cell phone to call Charles, but instead, she sent him a text saying, "*you wanna tell me about Veronica?*"

When Charles received the text from Giselle, he read it twice, thinking about how he should respond. At work, he asked his client to excuse him for just a moment. Charles walked out of the room and replied to Giselle, "*At work, we'll talk later; I'm with a client,*" which only gave him time to think. He must make sure he tells her the right thing because it can go way left. It depends on how well she receives reality versus her not wanting to see the truth. Judging from the fact that she even asked, lets him know she is at least open to allowing him to explain. About an hour later, once Charles finished with his sale, he reached out to Giselle and asked her to meet him at the Strat at six, and she replied, ok. The Strat's observation floor is a place that Charles frequently likes to go to; it has the best view of the entire valley and two because he can clear his mind. Being on the 108th and 109th floor is very serene, picturesque, and quiet. The lights of the strip casinos are beautiful and are as far as the eye can see. This discussion he is about to have with Giselle is either going to make them or break them, so his fingers are crossed.

They met at the top of the Strat and of course, not only is she looking ravishingly beautiful, she is, hands down, the sexiest woman in the world to him. It's a windy but clear night, so as they approach each other, he quickly reaches out to hug her, attempting to shield her from all the wind blowing and swirling her long locs of hair all around. It's the first time Charles has ever met up with her empty-handed, which he thought was best because he did not want to appear to be cheesy or presumptuous regarding their relationship. He said hello as he held her hands, and she looked him dead in his face with her bright Bambi eyes and replied with a solemn, heart hurting hey. He starts by saying, "Thank you for meeting with me. How was your day"? She said, "It was ok, but it could've been better." He licked his lips as he so often does, saying, "Well, you look gorgeous, as usual." She quickly shouts out, "Charles cut the crap, who is Veronica?!"

Charles took a deep breath and explained to Giselle, the woman he loves, why the woman he lost his daughter with is no longer a significant factor in his life. He did his best, to tell the truth as he sees it, hoping she would understand. Giselle feels pressed; the man standing before her is the man of her dreams. He is handsome, masculine, kind, thoughtful, smart, and by his accounts, he has not been intimate with Veronica since he and Giselle started seeing each other seriously. She doesn't want to make any rash decisions, so she tells him she needs to think about it, and they will talk later. All he could do is say ok and hope for the best. He walked her to her car, and they went their separate ways.

When Giselle arrived home, she went up to her room, and the first thing her eyes focused on was the plane tickets to the Caribbean Charles gave her for Christmas she kept on her dresser. As she lays on her bed, tears fall from her eyes as a million thoughts run through her mind. She thought Charles was "the one." He is hands down the best lover she has ever had, and he's also the most thoughtful and romantic man she has ever met. She replays his story over and over in her head until her teary eyes become weary and start to burn. She wants to shut everything out, so she closes her eyes and drifts off to sleep. Giselle tossed and turned throughout the night, and she woke up early the next morning with a heavy heart. Her dreams of getting married and having babies feel somewhat uncertain.

She thought long and hard over the next few hours about what the two of them have together, and for sure, she is not interested in being anyone's side chick. Charles sent her a text saying, "*Good morning beautiful, I hope you are having a good day. Follow your heart, I am here*". Dammit, Giselle thought, why does he have to be so damn lovable? She responds by saying, "*thank you, ttyl.*" She's feeling torn; on the one hand, Charles is the love of her life, but on the other hand, she doesn't want him to make a fool of her. After thinking about how hard it's been to meet him with the pickings of good men being so slim in sin city, she decides to give him a chance to see how things go. Overall, he's a good man, and he never did anything to hurt her in any way. Almost like clockwork, he sent her another text saying, "*you wanna meet for dinner tonight?*" and she replied, *yes.*

Giselle met Charles for dinner, and she had both copies of the trust with her so that she can talk with him about it. She showed him both documents and explained how the one that was implemented by Veronica is not legal or valid. In shock, he had no idea about this because he trusted Veronica. After clearly seeing the deception, he is determined to talk with Veronica about it and asks Giselle to please give him some time to speak to her, and she agreed. Charles felt terrible because he always thought Leilani was a good person, and now knowing she has Art's child, he feels the need to speak up. He asked Giselle what Leilani feels about it, and she said she doesn't believe Leilani even realizes there are two different trusts. Giselle thinks Leilani never even looked at either of the docs because both envelopes were sealed. As they eat dinner, he asks if she has decided anything about their relationship, and she told him not yet. She needs some time to think, but she will let him know soon.

When Charles arrived home, he immediately went into the bedroom to confront Veronica. He wants answers to specific questions, and what she says will determine what he plans to do. He asks, since they have incurred so many medical bills in such a short time, has she given any thought to maybe selling one of the properties. Blowing him off once again, she refuses and attempts to change the subject. Next, he goes in and also asks about the plane. He reminds her that she does not have an income, and holding on to that plane is just way too expensive. She replied, "You're right, it is costly, but I will lease it out. We don't use it that much, and people will pay a lot to use it, so we can afford to keep it." Then he asks her, "How much money is in the bank accounts?" Then she replied, "Why are you asking me so many questions?" He then asked, "So you're not going to tell me how much is in the bank accounts? She then said, "Look, the bank accounts are intact, and I haven't touched them, ok"? Shocked at what she just said, he knew for a fact that she has spent at least a million dollars, if not more, since Art died, and he was starting to become unhinged.

Feeling nervous, Veronica stood up and started to raise her voice just a little, and it rubs Charles the wrong way. He snapped and told her; all the years they've been together, he has been an open book, and right now, he doesn't like what's going on. She now screams at the top of her lungs, asking him what he needs to know? Charles shouted, "I want to know where you got the money for all the things you've been financing"! Feeling under pressure, to get him to shut up, and not thinking it through, she told him, "Look, Art had $3 million in cash in his wall safe". Charles looked at her in shock and said, "Ok, so how much is left, Veronica?" She said, "Ummmmm, not much." Charles yelled out, "What do you mean, not much? "Well, I had to give Tom, Arts attorney, $1million, I paid the surrogate and the hospital bill for the baby. I paid for all of my cancer bills, including my boob job, and I paid off that Tesla that you just gave me, so I have a few hundred thousand left.

Charles sat quietly for a moment, knowing what she just said didn't add up to three million dollars, so he asks why did she have to give Art's attorney a million dollars? Discombobulated, she looked at him and said, "What? You know what? I don't have to answer you! We're not married!

Get out! Get the hell out of here! I don't need you! I let you move into this beautiful house with me when you had nothing! You were just a bouncer at a damn club! I got you that job working for Art, and he was good to you, and he paid you well, but did you appreciate it? No, you want to stress me out over some dumb shit!". Charles looked at Veronica steadily while she was doing all that yelling.

He couldn't believe all the things she said, but he made a mental note of everything before he decided to respond. He heard all he needed to hear from her, and when she finally stopped, he said, "You know what? You're right; we aren't married. I thought we were deeper than this, but obviously, I'm wrong. You've said all I need to hear. I'll get my things, Veronica, and you won't have to deal with me." He walked away from her, and she stood there, stunned and unable to speak. She didn't want him to leave but thinks she may have said more than what she can take back as sorrowful tears start to well up in her eyes.

Chapter Five

Celebrate, Party and Travel

It's summer and one of Leilani's favorite things to do during the season is have a backyard barbeque. She hires a catering company to serve the food, but she likes to cook everything herself, so Tony helps her plan the menu. She ordered three cases of St Louis ribs, a fifty-pound beef brisket, ten whole chickens, and her family shipped ten pounds of authentic Louisiana sausages. The typical sides are collard greens, mac & cheese, potato salad, baked beans, and coleslaw, and Giselle made all the desserts, sweet potato pies, cheesecakes, cookies, and peach cobblers. As always, she hired a bartender with a fully stocked bar and assorted beverages for the kids. There are ten round tables of six with white tablecloths, and the music played inside the house and outback.

She invited about sixty people, including Tony's girlfriend, her daughter and niece, Giselle's Boo Charles, and Tony's good friend Hank of course. Knowing he would be there, Leilani made sure to look extra cute. As the guests begin to arrive and fill the backyard, Leilani surveys everything inside and out to make sure her guests are happy and everything is right. Hank walks up, greets her, and hands her a lovely bouquet of flowers and a bottle of good wine. While smiling and thanking him, he reaches in and gives her a full-body hug, holding on to her longer than expected, letting her know he missed her. Feeling his body so close to hers made her want to melt. Taking in a deep breath, he smells intoxicating, but she composes herself. The day is just starting, and if things go well, he might stay the night like he did the last time. Glad to see him as well, she squeezes him back in a slightly flirtatious way, and then he kisses her on both of her cheeks. Ooooh, she thought, his lips are so soft.

He looks all around her decorated backyard and then pans over to the tables where the BBQ favorites are in roll top chafing dishes on white tablecloths. Then he sees the full bar over to the left and, separate dessert table over to the right and says, "Wow, you sure give great parties," and he hugs her again. "Thank you, Hank; it's good to see you again." While he is holding both her hands, they continue to look into each other's eyes for an awkward moment, and then he finally let's go. His hands are big and strong with a soft touch like he knows what to do with them, and Leilani imagines how they would feel exploring all over her body. Little Arabella running around and playing, skips up to them, hangs on to Leilani's leg, and belts out a big hi to Hank. Surprised at how much she's grown, he bends down to greet her. "Well, hello there, Princess Arabella, how are you?" Blushing and giggling, she says, fine! He looks back up at Leilani and says, "She's beautiful." Smiling, she said, "Thank you. Come on, get something to eat", as she takes him by the hand and leads him over to the food.

This year she hired a local comedian and a female singer to perform, and everyone loved them. Some people are playing cards, some are playing dominoes, and some are dancing while others are sitting, drinking, talking, and eating. What matters most to Leilani is that everyone has a good time, and she can gauge it by the sounds of everyone's voices mixed in with the music. The sound of happy people enjoying themselves is like music to her ears. It's such a familiar sound from all those years working in the restaurants from her humble beginnings. Hanks' favorite song came on, so of course, he pulled Leilani to the dance floor to Cha Cha with him. They looked great swaying together and were very much in sync with each other. They were dancing so well, everyone started to notice and egged them on. Go, Lani, go, Hank, go, Lani, go, Hank, go, go, go, go, go, go! They danced to the next slow song, and as their bodies snuggly connected, she felt a strong and inviting chemistry with him.

As the afternoon sun turns into late night, most of the guests start to leave, but the usual crowd, including Hank, hangs around to chit chat and drink. Leilani knew this would be a very long day and night, so she has the sitter for Arabella to enjoy the rest of the evening. By the end of the night, everyone goes to their respective rooms, leaving Leilani and Hank alone. Very attracted to each other, the alcohol gave them both the courage to go for it. He grabs her face and kisses her mouth passionately. As their bodies embrace, he holds a loc of her hair. He then moves his hands down her shoulders, around to her back, squeezing her waist, and finally cupping her azz. As he kisses her neck, making her wet, she grabs his hands and says nothing as she guides him up the stairs into her bedroom.

Leilani always burns candles in her room, so when they walked in, not only does it smell amazing, but the ambient glow is just right for their mood. She turns on her favorite Jhene Aiko Pandora playlist, and they both walk to the bathroom and into the shower. Still kissing and caressing each other's bodies, they lather each other sensually. She is two years older than him, and his body is perfect in every way and judging from the way he kisses, she can tell she is in for a treat. After their refreshing shower, they dry each other off and walk to the bed. He lays her down and lies between her thighs, all the while still kissing each leg, working his way up. The time he takes to love her body, paying attention to every little detail, relaxes her. His lips feel soft as he slowly glides his tongue on her sweet spot. He masterfully surrounds her sweet lips with his tongue and lips in search of her clit as he gently sucks on it until she bursts with pleasure.

He doesn't know what level of kinkiness she wants to experience, but he's ready to explore phase two. They begin missionary style because he wants to look her in the eye, and he pumps his long and thick penis inside her reaching her g-spot, making her come again. Right at the last second, he climaxes, and she feels his climax pulsating inside her. He then turns her on her side, and scissor pumps her until she comes again. He gets her a hot, wet towel to clean the excess cum, and they lay together for a few minutes to catch their breaths.

She reaches over to go down on him, and he loves it. His penis is much larger than average, so she massages it with both hands. She licks up and down and all around until he releases another orgasm. He flips her around, stroking her doggy style, plunging in and out, fast and slow, while grabbing her ass. She is light as a feather weighing just over one hundred pounds, so he turns her around to face him. She holds onto his neck and straddles her legs around his waist as he scoops her up. He walks with her around the room, holding, pumping, and balancing her tiny body in his strong arms and hands with each stroke until they both explode and burst like fireworks again. He is in such great shape; he handles her with ease, and his deep strokes are like a well-choreographed dance performance. Every inch of his body is so muscular and healthy, so she feels secure, and she can tell she will be craving him relentlessly. They fell asleep, and just before sunrise, he woke up and got dressed. He reached over and kissed her face and told her he doesn't want Arabella to wake up and find him there. He said he'd call her later, and she said ok.

Charles found a decent three-bedroom rental not far from Leilani's house, so a lot of his free time is going shopping with Giselle to make it homey and habitable. Not much of a decorator, he gave her full range picking out most things because he wants her to be comfortable when she comes over. They start planning their Caribbean trip because they want to go before August to avoid the hurricane season. She is excited about going because this will be her first time traveling to the islands. Charles was born there and very familiar with the island life, so it's just returning home for him.

Their Caribbean trip is today, and she is excited about going with Charles, and because his family still lives there, she's looking forward to meeting them. It took her a minute to forgive him for Veronica, but she knows he's a good dude, plus she is addicted to the way he loves her. Most of his family lives in Barbados, but they started their trip to Grenada's spice island. Only about one hundred fifty miles from Barbados, it's a French colonized culture, so Giselle felt right at home. They have a breathtakingly beautiful view at the five-star Orchard Bay Villa, and as soon as they walk in, Giselle is in heaven. They enjoyed lots of water sport activities and went to Gouyve for fish Friday. It's a big celebration of locals and visitors enjoying all kinds of grilled fish, starting right around six pm. After eating tons of grilled fish, they walked along the beach to take in the sunset. The next day they chartered a sailboat to explore Sandy island, and later that night, they attended the Grenada Music festival to listen to reggae, with Joss Stone as the headline performer.

Early the next morning, after eating at the Creole Shack, they scheduled a guided tour at Laura's Spice Garden, and later they ate lunch and then drove to River Antoine Rum Distillery for dinner that night. The following day, they went to Morne Rouge Beach in St George and explored the beautiful coral reefs and the Underwater Sculpture Park. They spent the entire next day at Grand Anse, the largest beach in Grenada. They took a charter flight over to Barbados the next day so Giselle could meet his family, and they loved her. His mom, aunt, uncles, and little cousins were all there, and they visited with them for most of the day. This was a timeless trip for them, so they didn't wear watches; they gaged their time by the sun's rising and setting each day. They have lots of great pictures that capture the memories, and the love they made will be forever in Giselle's heart. Making love with Charles in such a beautiful tropical environment made her feel special, and she wants to come back as often as they can. Saying goodbye to their tropical paradise, they slept most of the way on their nonstop flight home from Miami, feeling refreshed and getting back to their Vegas grinds.

Once home, Giselle and Charles talked about how to handle Art's trust and think it's best to speak with Veronica about it first. That way, maybe they can avoid risking Leilani filing a big lawsuit. Charles sent Veronica text messages asking to meet with him, but she never answered. After his third attempt to get her to meet up with him, he warns her to please respond because it has to do with Arts "legal" trust. She responded about five minutes later, *saying she is out of town and will get back with him as soon as she returns,* and he replied, ok. It allowed her time to think about how to deal with her fate and what she knows can ultimately blow up in her face.

Hank asked Leilani to have dinner at Lakeside at Wynn, and she gladly accepts. After their delicious dinner, they walked over to the showroom to see the all-water Cirque-like show Le Reve and loved it. His birth name is Henok Tesfaye, but growing up, all his friends called him Hank. He's been in Vegas since the age of twenty and was born in Rehoboth Beach, Delaware. Leilani has never met anyone from Delaware, so she is curious about what it's like growing up there. She is intrigued by his family dynamic and understands the challenges he must've faced growing up in a multi-racial family as she did. His parents and two younger sisters still live there, and he tells her all about growing up in the small east coast beach town, and he also told her about his favorite surrounding cities: Fenwick Island, Cape Henlopen, and Ocean City.

His mom is from Bengaluru, Karnataka, the Capitol Region of Southern India, and his dad is from Addis Ababa, which is the largest capital city of Ethiopia. Both of his parents have very dark skin, and why he also has a beautiful dark complexion. His parents met in college at the University of Delaware, and they both graduated with Engineering degrees and married not long after. Hank, their oldest, was born two years later, and then his twin sisters were born just five years after him. He told her he'd love to take her there whenever she wants, and she's looking forward to it and can't wait. Hank earns a good salary as a Senior Executive Casino Host for one of the larger strip casinos where he and Tony met. He loves his job and enjoys all the added perks.

Very outgoing, Hank knows all the hot spots of Vegas, plays golf at the best courses with his high roller clients, and dines with them at the better restaurants throughout the Valley. He speaks three languages, is strikingly handsome, very well connected, and is a world traveler. Working in the hospitality industry in Vegas has allowed him to experience the finer things in life despite being such a young man in his late twenties. Originally his parents were skeptical and disappointed that he dropped out of college and relocated to Vegas. Still, he quickly excelled within the industry, so they are happy and very proud of his success.

His work schedule is extremely demanding, but he always makes a special effort to spend as much time with Leilani as he can. Like most men in their late twenties, he has a very high sex drive, and since Leilani's schedule is more flexible, they often manage to see each other at odd times. Day and night, she loves the time spent with him because he always makes it exciting, making her crave him. His tastefully decorated home in Summerlin is smaller than Leilani's, but she likes being there with him just as much as he enjoys being at her house. Because of their flexible schedules, he would text her to meet for a little afternoon delight. They took turns meeting at each other's homes, made mad, passionate love, and then go back to their workplaces. It's not the usual dating method, but their chemistry is so undeniable that they can't get enough of each other. Hank keeps his home very clean, and it's well decorated. He has framed art and sculptures from his world travels in every room. His master suite is significantly large, so his bed is placed triangularly in the middle of the room, not against any walls, which Leilani thinks is sexy and unique. She has never seen anyone arrange their furniture in the way he does, and she loves his décor taste and style.

Hank is quite a catch and has lived an exciting bachelor's life since he's been in Vegas over the years, but now he is ready to settle down so he can start a family, and he believes Leilani and Arabella are perfect for him. He digs her calm and loving spirit, and he loves how she always makes him feel special and needed. She is strikingly beautiful, and he loves how amazing she is with Arabella. Watching how she cares for her makes him want her to be the mother of his children. They love their time together; they get along well, and they have similar beliefs and goals in life. They are both financially stable, have a great sex life, and love to travel. They are both easy going and love to chill, so they don't fight or argue. After losing Art the way Leilani did, she didn't think she would ever meet another man that was anything like him, but now after being with Hank and knowing how amazing he is, she is happy to be wrong. She is very attracted to him, and she loves how he is with Arabella. He is a kind and loving man who is taking the grief of losing Art out of her broken heart, giving her a new outlook on life.

Because they both play golf, Hank planned a quick trip to Palm Springs for the weekend for the two of them. He likes to drive instead of flying because the four-hour road trip helps him unwind. Leilani left Arabella at home with Giselle and the babysitter to enjoy some one on one time for the weekend. Leilani was surprised when Hank picked her up in a brand-new, custom Range Rover that he bought through Charles. She didn't realize the two of them had become friends since Arabella's birthday party back in February, but it's beautiful. Hank, Tony, and Charles all have become friends since then. Hank is very attentive to Leilani; he has their favorite drinks and snacks already in the car. Hank holds and kisses Leilani's hand while the two talk about their future while listening to her favorite playlist of Jhene Aiko on Pandora. He's a good driver, and they arrive in Palm Springs around one o'clock.

He booked a suite at the JW Marriott Desert Springs Resort & Spa in Palm Desert. From the moment they stepped into the lobby, they were amazed at the exquisiteness of the property. Even though it's their first time traveling to this resort, it felt just like being home. The entire property is breathtakingly gorgeous with beautiful mountain views. It sits on a full golf course, with several restaurants, a spa and gym, grass tennis courts, gondola boats on the lake full of beautiful flamingos, and several pools and Jacuzzis. Leilani loves the whole Palm Springs vibe because it's a desert paradise just like Vegas, but it also has that small town, nostalgic, laid-back kind of feel. She suggests maybe Tony and his girlfriend Isabella would like to join them the next time they come out; Hank agreed and then said, "yes, maybe your cousin Giselle and her man Charles can come out as well." Standing behind her, he wraps his arms around her waist, softly kisses her neck, and whispers in her ear; but for right now, miss lady, it's just you and me. Let's get this weekend started!

It's still early in the day, and the room won't be ready for at least another hour or two, so they explore the resort and take it all in. Returning to the lobby, they got the keys and went up to a high floor room overlooking the golf course and mountains. They unpack, kiss, and get in a quickie, freshen up and go back downstairs to get a bite to eat at the Daily Grill on El Paseo. They went back west through Palm Springs on highway 10 over to the outlets for a little shopping after lunch. Before returning to the resort, they took the Aerial Tram to catch Coachella Valley's spectacular views. That evening after dinner at Rio Azul, they walked downtown on south Palm Canyon Drive at the Thursday night street fair. Back at the resort, they felt a little fatigued, but not too much to make love. Hank insatiably craves Leilani and leaves no part of her body untouched or unkissed, and she loves every minute of being with him. After their first love session, they take a nap for just about an hour, then get up, shower, and make love all over again.

Just before sunrise, they get ready for their six a.m. tee time on the course, and after he beat her in golf, they went back to the resort room for more sex, another shower, and a nap. When they woke up from their nap, they made love again before going to the Spa Agua Caliente Casino for a little gambling just for fun. After a couple of hours at the casino, they had a taste for Greek, so he took her to Miro's on South Palm Canyon Drive, and they enjoyed a nice Mediterranean dinner on the patio.

The next day, she takes the wheel and drives out to BSG, her Santa Monica restaurant. He's never been there, so she wanted to show him a little bit of her world. Right now, she's in the middle of negotiations with a buyer, hoping to finalize it soon. She may not travel here again any time soon, so she wanted to check on things. The ride took about an hour and a half, and she's surprised at how different east LA looked along the 10-freeway headed westbound into Santa Monica. It felt strange and vaguely familiar driving in from that direction, and she is happy that she lives in Vegas. Everything looks much older than she remembered, and it feels weird. When they arrived, Hank thought her restaurant was beautiful. They sat down to eat, and he loved everything he had. Looking at Leilani proudly, he felt sad she's deciding to sell it, but he's ok with it since she's ok with it.

After dinner, Leilani took Hwy 1 to Malibu, then connected to the 101 freeway at the San Fernando Valley's west end. She got off the freeway and took Ventura Blvd through Woodland Hills, Tarzana, Sherman Oaks, and turned right on Hayvenhurst to show him where the Jackson's used to live. Continuing along Ventura Blvd through Encino, they turned right on

Sepulveda, down past the Getty. She then hopped on the 405 Fwy at Sunset and took the 10 Fwy eastbound back to Palm Desert to the Marriott. It was a very long day, so when they finally got up to the room, they dived on the bed and fell asleep. After a few hours, Leilani wakes up and gets in the tub for a nice, luxurious bubble bath. Moments later, feeling her absence, Hank climbs in the tub with her, caressing and loving on her, and finish with another love session in the bedroom. Late the next morning, room service delivered them a delicious Continental breakfast. Chillin and wearing white terrycloth robes, they ate breakfast in bed while watching tv and made love one more time for the road. Afterward, they packed, showered, said goodbye to the Coachella Valley, and headed back home to Vegas.

Veronica is back in town and finally responded to Charles, saying they can meet up, so he met her at the house. They exchange hellos, and with her guard up, the first thing she said to him was, "So you need to speak with me about Art's trust.? Are you trying to get money out of me"? Charles looked at her sideways and said, "No, Veronica, I'm not trying to get money out of you, but how have you been"? Relieved, she told him her breast implants have been bothering her, so she may need to get them replaced. Not wanting her to get them in the first place, he told her he was sorry to hear about that.

In response, Veronica let her guard down a little more and told him she's running out of money, so she's been a little irritated about it lately. Charles is just looking at her, wondering how she could be so cruel and greedy. He read the entire original trust. It was clear Art wanted everything to go to Leilani, and Veronica was supposed to get one hundred thousand dollars, which is more than what any employer would give to an employee. She continued to make small talk as he listened, and finally, he couldn't take it anymore and explained why he was there. He handed her a copy of the original trust, and she immediately stood up and abruptly said, "Where did you get this?!" He looked her dead in the face and said, "Never mind where I got it from; what matters is who else has a copy of it. "Veronica, what were you thinking?"

She paused for a very long time and explained in detail how she just felt so left out. She told Charles she did so many things to help Art make lots of money over the years. She felt insulted, and it was like a slap in the face for him just to give her that measly little hundred thousand dollars. She went on and on about why he should've given her so much more. She knew Leilani wouldn't have contested it, so she gave Tom one million dollars to rewrite the adjoining pages to show her as the primary beneficiary and not Leilani. She asked, "Is she complaining or something? She got millions from the life insurance policy. What else does she want? Are you with her or something? Why are you so involved in this anyway?" At this point, she's ranting and raving again, pacing back and forth, filled with anger and upset. Charles then asks, "Well, didn't you get some of the insurance money too?" More enraged, she didn't realize he knew about the insurance money, so she shut down and got quiet.

Charles calmly looks at her and asks, "So you gave Tom one million dollars? That's what was in the briefcase when we were at the airport?" "Yes, Veronica said. I gave it to him in cash, and that's why he went to Mexico." Wanting to see if she would lie or tell the truth, Charles said, "But where did you get that kind of money to give to him? Art had just died, and the insurance company hadn't even paid out yet. She looked at Charles and said, "Art kept quite a bit of cash in his safe at the house? Well, I used that money. That's how I've been able to pay all these bills, the money from the safe. I don't have a job. How else was I supposed to live?" Charles shook his head and said, "So how much money was in the safe?" Veronica said, "Look, I already told you months ago, he had a few million in cash in the safe." Nervously she again said, "How the hell do you think I have been paying for all these bills and expenses, Charles? Do you think I just pulled the cash out of my ass?" Then Charles interjected and said, "But what about the insurance money? What happened to that money?" Veronica said, "I gave it to my foster dad to buy more gas stations in Cleveland. He sends me money every month."

Trying to remain calm, Charles approached her and said, "Look, Veronica, I understand how you feel, and you're right; Art should've given you more than he did, but the fact is he didn't. I think you should've done this differently." Smirking, Veronica said, "Really, Charles, do you believe Leilani would've given me any of that money? Oh please, give me a break; we're in the real world here; people don't just give people money like that, especially incompetent bitches like her! There are two kinds of people in this world; givers and takers, and I'm not interested in anyone taking from me! I'm a survivor, and I did what was best for me! I worked hard for Art, and I deserved more than that measly hundred thousand dollars!" Charles asks, "So how much money did you get from the insurance company Veronica?" She mumbled, "We both got a few million dollars." Charles raised his eyebrows in shock and said, "So you got millions from the insurance company, plus the money in the safe?" He's looking at her in disbelief. He had no idea she was this heartless and greedy.

He quickly stood up and said, "Veronica, I know Art's properties are all paid off, so you've been living off the rent from the tenant in the guest house, which was fifteen hundred a month. Then you have the Air B & B money from the Hamptons house, which is thousands a month. You also get the rent from the four condos in Santa Monica, plus you're getting money from some gas stations you just said your foster dad sends. Oh, and come to think of it, you rent out the jet, so you're also making money from that! All that put together is quite a bit every month. I didn't even mention the revenue you will get from the cannabis farm in a minute. What you produce from the farm alone will rake in millions for you every month. Come on now, Veronica, how much money do you need? I'm trying to help you out here!"

He looked Veronica dead in the face and said, "Do you know Leilani can take you to court and sue the shit out of you at the very least? What's much worse, you could go to jail for what you did! Again, I say, what were you thinking?" Veronica replied, "So what Charles, is that what she wants to do, sue me? Are you with her or something"? "No, Veronica, I'm not with her, but you need to fix this because the truth is not in your favor. This shit is going to blow up in your face, and all I'm saying is, you gotta figure out what you're going to do. I read over the entire trust. What were you planning to do with all the properties, the stocks, the bonds, and the plane? What was your plan?" Now, in tears and about to break down, Veronica said, "Well, if Leilani ever figured it out and wanted to sue me, I figured I'd make enough money from the cannabis farm to pay her back. I'm here all by myself with no one to turn to or to help me. You left me like I was nothing to you, but I am going to figure something out."

Now Charles feels it's time for a little disclosure. "First of all, I didn't just leave you Veronica; you kicked me out, remember? Secondly, did you know Leilani had Art's, baby? She has a little girl, and she looks exactly like him". Veronica could not believe her ears. She turned and looked at him, seething with envy, and shouted, "What? How do you know that"? He then pulled out his cell phone and showed her a picture of Arabella, and Veronica looked as though she was looking at a ghost. Veronica continued to stare at Arabella's picture in disbelief. "Veronica, don't you think Art's only child should be apart of his estate?" With her mind racing. In doubt, Veronica asks, "How old is she, Charles?" "She was born on February fourteenth last year, the day Alayna died." Now, in shock, Veronica's eyes widen and begin to fill with tears. Feeling dizzy, she starts to fall to the floor, but he caught her. Charles picked her up, carried her to the spare bedroom, and gently laid her on the bed. He put a cold towel on her forehead and stayed with her until she was coherent.

A few minutes later, she opened her eyes as he was stroking her ' hair and whispering sweetly to her, saying things would be ok. Once she got her composure, he continued their conversation and told her he believes Leilani would've given her money if she had just asked. Veronica stayed quiet and just asked him to please give her some time to process it all, and he said he couldn't make her any promises, but he would try. He asked, "Look, are you going to be ok? Do you need me to get you anything? I gotta go; I'll check on you tomorrow." "No, she said I'll be ok, you can go," and he left. That picture of Arabella is burning a hole in Veronica's heart, and can't get her beautiful face out of her head. She is so sad about losing Alayna; she feels grief-stricken, reliving the pain all over again.

When Charles arrived home, Giselle was there waiting for him, and she asked how it went? He shook his head, saying, "not so good, but I need to talk with her again because right now, she's trippin." "Trippin, how?" Giselle asked. "Come on, he said, let's go sit down," and he began to explain. "Veronica is a broken woman. I can see that she is on the brink of a mental breakdown or something. I confronted her about everything, and she just needs a little time to get herself together. Let's give her some time, and I'll go back to her to explain what's going to happen. "Have you talked with Leilani about it yet"? "No, Giselle said, I haven't, but I'm not going to wait too long. She deserves to know the truth, especially for Arabella". "Yeah, I get it, let's just give her a little time. I'll reach out to her in a couple of weeks". "Ok, babe, if you think that's best, then I'll wait two weeks. I won't say anything to Leilani about it, but hopefully, Veronica will get her act together by then".

Leilani hasn't been feeling herself lately and is starting to feel a bit queasy, so she sips a little seven up in the mornings to settle her stomach. Almost two now, Arabella is as cute as she can be, getting into everything and keeping Leilani on her toes. Leilani usually has a lot of energy, but lately, she tires easily. She missed her period last month, so she's contemplating taking a pregnancy test. She went to the drug store, bought one of those home pregnancy kits, peed on the stick, and was surprised that it came out positive. Nervous, she immediately called her doctor and made an appointment. One week later, her doctor confirmed that she is indeed pregnant. Heavy in thought, she thought about how and when she was going to tell Hank. They have date plans for tonight, and she's thinking about telling him on their date.

Later that evening, Hank picks Leilani up and drives north towards downtown. Puzzled, she wondered where they could be going, but knowing how connected he is about places to go in Vegas, she didn't need to ask. He pulls into the Four Queens, and they walk through the casino and head downstairs to Hugo's Cellar, an old school, romantic steakhouse. Right away, they were greeted by a host wearing a tuxedo who presented Leilani with a single-stemmed, red rose. They were then escorted to their table and received menus. The sommelier stepped to their table and suggested the perfect wine once they placed their orders. They had a variety of warm bread with rose-shaped butter. Their salads were prepared tableside, and they each got a spoonful of sorbet to cleanse their palates between servings. They both enjoyed steak and lobster superbly prepared along with delectable sides. Chocolate covered strawberries, apricots, and baby figs are served after dinner as a sweet treat.

Just as they finished eating the sweets, Hank slid his hand across the table, holding a ring box. As Leilani opened it, he said, "Will you marry me?" Shocked at the gorgeousness of the ring, she looked at him and said, yes! He told her he'd dated many women over the years but never met anyone quite like her and knows he wants her in his life forever. Her heart is smiling. She adores this man and is looking forward to a beautiful life with him. She's thinking now is the perfect time to tell him. "Babe, I'm pregnant." Shocked and amazed, he replied, "What? Wow, this must be my lucky day!" He stands up, walks over, wraps his arms around her, and they kiss. They left the restaurant and went to his house, and the two of them made love like there was no tomorrow. As usual, they kissed each other from head to toe leaving nothing unloved or untouched. Hank's attraction and desire for Leilani are unwavering and relentless, and he never hesitates to show her just how much he cares, and she could not be happier.

It's now been two weeks, so Giselle urges Charles to get back with Veronica because she is anxious about getting the right outcome for her cousin. Charles goes back over to Veronica's house to see if she knows what to do. Veronica begs Charles to give her the chance to make some money from her cannabis farm before talking with Leilani, which will provide her with the opportunity to have a decent life. He asked her how much more time she needed, and she said, "give me sixty days." Her first harvest is just about ready, and she will literally have enough to start a new life; and she's even thinking about moving to Colorado, so she can try to forget about all of this. "See, Charles, I could leave everything here, and it can just all go back to Leilani. I just need to make some money to start my new life". Charles said, "Ok, I'll get back with you."

He calls Giselle at work and tells her Veronica is asking for sixty days to make enough money to start a new life somewhere else and urges her just to let the woman get her life together and move on. That way, Leilani will get everything she is supposed to get, and then they all will be done with her, and Giselle said ok. Charles suggests they go out for a little comedy and have some dinner, and she said ok. He took her to Hank's Fine Steaks and Martinis. They had appetizers of crab cakes, oysters Rockefeller, and lobster chowder. For their main entrees, Charles had a grass-fed filet mignon, and Giselle had a rib eye. Giselle is falling asleep in her seat, and Charles taps the table saying, "Babe am I that boring?" "No, Gisselle said, sorry babe, I'm just tired; it's been a long day." He said, "Come on, let's go. I'm going to take you home so you can get some rest." Instead of taking her home, he drove to his house. Giselle was too tired to object, so they went inside and went to sleep. In the middle of the night, with Giselle spooned right next to him, Charles got horny, so of course, he starts kissing on her neck, then turns her over and kisses her breast, which awakes and arouses her, so she reciprocates, and they quietly make love until the sun rises.

It's the end of October, and as the blazing summer heat finally leaves for winter to take over, Giselle is almost done shopping for the annual December to Remember Christmas event. She loves this part of her job, and it allows her to make some great memories for the kids at the center. Leilani has a doctor's appointment, and Hank goes with her. She gets prepped for an ultrasound sonogram to view the baby growing inside her belly. As the nurse probes her stomach, she announces she is pregnant with twin girls, and they should be arriving in mid-summer! "Oh, my goodness, Leilani exclaimed; it looks like we hit the jackpot!" The look on Hank's face is priceless, and he couldn't be happier, saying, "Wow, now I'll have three little girls. What a blessing; as he reached over and kissed Leilani on the lips, they both smile, full of anticipation. Just then, Leilani gets a call from a Utah number. She doesn't know anyone in Utah, so she ignored the call and sent it to voicemail. She wants to tell Giselle and Tony the exciting news of having twins, but instead, she decided to wait a while.

The December to Remember at the center was a huge success, and now Leilani makes plans for Arabella's second birthday party. As her belly is starting to get bigger and she is no longer able to hide the obvious, Giselle asks her if she was pregnant. "Yes, Leilani beamed with joy, but please don't say anything. Hank and I are having a New Year's Eve get together at the house, and we will announce it then." "Ok, Giselle said, I'll act like I'm surprised."

Giselle and Leilani are running around getting the last-minute details for the party. A variety of foods and beverages are in the kitchen and dining areas, and a couple dozen of their closest friends were all enjoying the music, food, and festivities. As usual, Leilani hired a local comedian to do a stand-up session at the party. Just as he finished his routine, Leilani and Hank announced they are engaged to be married and pregnant at about eleven forty-five. Everyone hugged each other, shouted, and cheered and congratulated them. Hank kissed Leilani under the mistletoe and started the new year full of anticipation of babies and marriage, whichever comes first.

They decided to have a gender reveal at Arabella's birthday party. She's two, and Leilani had the party at home just like the last time, but this time there were more guests because Hank's friends are attending. After Arabella's birthday celebration, a drone flew overhead, and everyone directed their attention up. Hank announces they have a special delivery, and at the count of three, the drone released hundreds of pink rose petals, and the guests cheered. As a second drone flew overhead, Leilani said, "Wait, it looks like we have a second drone; everyone, please look back up!" Just then, the second drone released another set of pink rose petals, and Hank held up a blown-up picture of the sonogram of their twin daughters, and the crowd cheered even louder, which was super touching.

Hank asks Leilani if she and Arabella will take a short trip to Delaware with him. He wants his family to meet them, plus he's excited about having twins, and of course, she said yes. The three of them caught a flight to Wicomico Regional Airport in Salisbury, Maryland. Arabella did well on the plane as Hank and Leilani kept her occupied and entertained, so she didn't make any fusses. When they arrived at his parent's house, all his family were there. His parents, cousins, aunts, uncles, and twin sisters were all excited to see them and welcomed Leilani and Arabella with loving and open arms. Leilani was happy to see and meet them all, and it was just like when she went to New Orleans to meet her dad's family. His mom speaks with a heavy Southern Indian accent, and his dad has an Ethiopian accent. Hank has a very slight accent, and she observed him communicating with his dad in Amharic and with his mom in Telugu with ease. After seeing Hank interact with both his parents in their native languages, Leilani wants to give their daughter's native names of his parent's origin, and Hank is touched.

There was an array of delectable foods that Leilani had never eaten before, but she was anxious to try them all. His mom prepared Malabar parotta, a flatbread topped with spicey beef, Vadas, savory donuts, Biryani, a beautifully colored yellow pilaf, and they also had Tandoori and curries. Most southern Indian cuisines use red dried chilies, fresh green chilies, coconut, tamarind, plantain, ginger, and garlic. His dad also prepared some traditional Ethiopian dishes, somewhat spicier like; Kategna, a spicy flatbread, Alecha, a milder spicey chicken stew seasoned with green ginger, and Tibs, sliced lamb pan-fried in butter, garlic, and onions. Leilani loved all the variety of new dishes his family served, and his mom gave her some recipes to make when they return home. Hank comes from a very loving family, and they all made Leilani and Arabella feel welcomed and accepted them both into the family. His parents put them up in one of their spare bedrooms, and the three of them slept in the same king-size bed, and they were comfortable.

The next day, Hank took Leilani and Arabella to drive down to Ocean City, Maryland, about an hour away. They took lots of pictures, walked along the boardwalk, shopped, visited Ripley's Believe it or Not Museum, and ate lunch. They returned to Rehoboth before sunset to hang out with his family. His younger twin sisters are beautiful, and they are a combination of both his parents. Looking at them, Leilani wonders if her twins will look more like his family or hers. Everyone in his family's complexions is a variety of cinnamon, cocoa brown, and deep dark chocolate hues.

In contrast, her Creole family are all very light-skinned and often mistaken for white in Louisiana's bayous. These babies will have a loving, rich family culture to learn from, and Leilani is full of anticipation. The next morning, they all said their goodbyes and gave each other lots of hugs and promises to visit soon for the wedding, and Leilani told them she couldn't wait to see them all again.

On their flight home, Leilani expressed to Hank how nice it was to meet his family, and she's looking forward to them all coming out for the wedding. He agreed and said, "Yes, me too, because **none** of them have ever been out to Vegas, so this will be like a two and one vacation for them." Arabella fell asleep just after taking off, and the two of them talk about how they want their wedding to be. They agree on a small ceremony with their closest family and friends, no more than one hundred people. Hank asks her if she would like to have her family from Louisiana come out, and she said yes, but she's not sure if they all can come out, but it's ok they'll have an experienced videographer to capture all the moments, and she will send copies to whoever can't make it out. They agree to pay for everything together, and they discuss colors and themes. Hank is flexible and tells her whatever she wants is cool with him. They haven't set a date, so Hank asks Leilani if she wants to get married before or after the baby's birth. "Let's wait until after I give birth so that they can be at the wedding." She doesn't know how big she will be carrying twins; either way, she doesn't want to be pregnant at their wedding. Hank laughs and says, "yeah, I get it, whatever you want, babe."

Giselle is at work thinking about how Veronica's sixty days are almost up, so she calls Charles to ask if she is making any progress in rebuilding her new life. He assures her, no matter what, it will get resolved. The office's receptionist answers a call from Highland Ridge Hospital in Utah asking to speak with Leilani for the third time. The receptionist told the person on the line she is out of town but will return tomorrow. They left a message and said they would call back. Giselle kept a mental note of it and went on with her day. Not feeling herself lately, Giselle is going to the bathroom more and wakes up feeling a little nauseous., so she took a pregnancy test, and it was positive. She loves Charles, and she can't wait to tell him, Leilani, and her big brother Tony the good news.

With Leilani having Arabella, the wedding, and twins on the way, Isabella's daughter Gabriella, and Giselle and Charles having a baby, the group is growing. Hank returning home to Vegas, connects with Tony at the casino. They chop it up, and he tells Tony how well everything went with

Leilani and Arabella meeting his family. Tony's girlfriend, Isabella, is from the Bronx, so she has that sexy Latina east coast accent. Her mother is from Columbia, and her dad is from Puerto Rico, and they met in the Bronx, where they both still live. Isabella is stunningly beautiful and is a classically trained dancer, so after graduating high school, she moved to Vegas to pursue a professional dance career.

Chapter Six

Blending Families

Leilani, back home from Delaware, goes into the office at the center to check on things. She chatted with the staff and showed them all the pictures from her trip, and they were happy that she is getting married and expanding her family. Checking her messages, Leilani sees there are several from that Utah number. Puzzled yet curious, she decided to return the call and spoke with Jane, the administrator. Leilani detected a seriousness in her voice as she listened to why she was calling. The lady told her they have a patient at their facility who's been there for quite some time. She explained the gentleman was previously in a coma, recovering from a brain injury for at least a year, before being admitted to their facility. The few statements he made were in French, and he didn't know his name. After months of therapy, he slowly began to reveal details about himself, so the staff became eager to identify him through traditional means.

They didn't know where he was from, but he was initially brought to the hospital by a homeless group due to his severe injuries. The administrator explained, "he's in fair health and recently started talking about her. After he recovered from his brain injury at the hospital, his behavior was often combative. He said things the staff either didn't believe or could understand; therefore, he transferred to their facility. Because he was brought to the hospital by homeless people, they assumed him to be homeless and mentally challenged. He continued to mention that he was a wealthy man but couldn't say anything believable to our staff."

She went on to say, "After repeatedly saying your name, the staff documented it. After doing an internet search, we obtained your cell number. After getting no response, we linked your name to the center and began calling there as well.". Leilani apologized and explained that she did get a few calls, but since she didn't know anyone in Utah, she opted not to answer the calls. At this point, Leilani expressed concern asking, "So you still don't know his name?" No, the administrator said, so Leilani asked her if she could please take a picture of the man and send it to her. She said yes, and would fax it right away. Leilani thanked her and would certainly follow up and ended the call. Perplexed, Leilani went to Giselle and told her about the conversation she had with the woman. "Wow, what a bizarre story, Giselle said; who do you think that man is?" "I have no idea Leilani said; I don't know anyone in Utah."

Moments later, the fax was buzzing in, and Leilani and Giselle both went over to it to see who the man was. As the paper slowly slid out of the fax machine, the man's face slowly reveals. In shock, Leilani nearly dropped to her knees. It was Art! But how could that be? The plane company said the crash had no survivors! "Oh my God, Giselle shouted, that's him?" Leilani said, "Well, he looks older. I can see he's lost a lot of weight, his head is shaved, but that looks like Art to me! I need to get him! I gotta go to

Utah!" Giselle asked if she wanted her to go along, and Leilani said, "No, please get Arabella from the daycare and take her home if I'm not back in time, I should go alone." A million and one things are running through her mind as she drove home. Tears ran down her face, feeling panicked and excited at the same time. Shaking and anxious, she called Hank and told him about the conversation she had, and he told her to slow down and wait for him to take her first thing in the morning because it's at least a five-hour drive, so she said ok.

As soon as Leilani left the office, Giselle immediately called Charles and told him the news. "You have got to be kidding me!" he said. "No, Giselle said, they faxed a picture of him." Charles said, "Take a picture of the fax and text it to me so I can see it," and she did. When Charles received Giselle's text message, he was unbelievably shocked and stared at the picture for a long time. Charles told Giselle that Art is a good dude and always did right by him. He missed Art tremendously, but glad he's still alive.

Now Charles is thinking about what Veronica is going to do. She spent his money and will now most likely have to pay it back, He's thinking about how much trouble she's in and wants to tell her, but for now, he's going to keep this information to himself until he figures out the best thing to do. He told Giselle to keep him posted, and she said ok and ended the call. Then Giselle called Tony to tell him what's going on, and Tony tells Giselle Hank is calling on the other line, and he'll get back to her. Hank tells Tony that he just got a call from Leilani saying Art is still alive, and he needs to take her to Utah first thing in the morning, and he wants him to go. Tony replied, "Yeah, Giselle was just telling me about that. It sounds crazy, but I'm off tomorrow, so we all should go." Hank thanked Tony and said there is no way he would let Leilani drive to Utah alone, and Tony agreed. Tony called Giselle back and told her he's going with Hank and Leilani to Utah first thing in the morning because family should be with her, and Giselle said she's going too.

When Leilani got to the house, she went to her closet and took out a big box of pictures of them together during happy times. She thinks if Art sees happier times, it would hopefully help with his memory. Leilani packed all the pictures of him away since she's been with Hank because he doesn't need to see photos of Art in her home. She laid on the bed and looked at dozens of pictures, and decide to take them all. A decade of friendship thought to be gone forever is resurfacing and feeling bittersweet. They shared so many beautiful memories, and she reflects on those good times. If Art had never gone missing and been declared dead, she believes the two of them would have been together. As she feels the butterfly-like movements of her twin girls in her belly, she can't ignore the fact that she has a new life with Hank, and they will soon be married. How could she explain all of this to Art.? Will he even understand all that has happened? After looking at all those pictures of the two of them, she cried herself to sleep.

A few hours later, Giselle arrived home, she put Arabella in her room to play, then went straight to Leilani's room, and they hugged. About an hour later, Tony arrived home, and he hugged Leilani as well, then

Hank pulled up, and they all talked and planned for the trip in the morning. Giselle called Charles to chat and told him she's going with Leilani, Tony, and Hank in the morning. He told her ok, wished Leilani well, and to be safe. Giselle had food delivered, and they all ate and talked about what happened today. The next morning, they dropped Arabella at the center's daycare, and the four of them went to Midvale, Utah, to see about Art. The facility was smaller than they all expected, only two floors, straightforward and dorm-like, but none of them have ever been to any mental facilities anyway, so what do they know? Leilani feeling nervous, Hank reaches over to kiss her to try and calm her nerves. They walk in together, and Leilani went to speak with the administrator as the three waited in the lobby.

The administrator walked Leilani to the back where the patients are, and Leilani carrying the box of photos follows her. As they walked into the room, Art was lying on his bed, and as soon as he looked up at Leilani, his eyes beamed with joy immediately. Overcome with so many emotions, Leilani walked over and hugged him. Even though he lost a lot of weight and wearing a buzz cut, there was no doubt she knew it was him. She thanked the administrator and sat down to talk with him. Art told Leilani how happy he was to see her, and she could not stop the tears from running down her face. He asked her what was in the box, so she immediately opened it, telling him the staff told her he had no memory, so she brought the pictures to help him try and remember things about his life. Art told Leilani he had been telling all the staff about his life, but no one believed him because he originally arrived as a John Doe from the hospital. He did suffer some memory loss, but because he had no identification and couldn't prove his identity, they thought he was crazy and transferred him there.

"Wow, Leilani thought. You've been here all this time"? "No, he said, the plane wrecked, and Philippe didn't make it. It took me days to get to a live person, and I thought I was dying. I stayed with some homeless people for a while because I distinctively remember them, and I believe they took me to the hospital. After coming out of the coma, the staff later told me everything that happened. Once I started to remember things, I tried to tell them who I was and what kind of life I had, but no one believed me, and then I ended up here. I have gotten extensive rehabilitation from this place. It's not just physical; it's mental as well". "Wow, Leilani said, you seem ok to me. I want to see if I can get you discharged so you can come home. But let me ask you, Art, how long do you think you were with the homeless people"? Art said, "Quite a while, but I'm not real sure exactly." Leilani then said, "Well, do you think it was a day, a week, or months"? Art said with a hurtful and sad face, "Months, I'm not sure how many," Hearing that made Leilani cry all over again.

After that, she walked out to speak with the administrator to see if she can get Art discharged. She showed her all the pictures of the two of them, and the lady said, there is just the matter of paying the bill, which is relatively high, and Leilani said, "No problem, whatever the account is, I will pay it." The lady then said, "Ok, give me until tomorrow to draft all the necessary paperwork and process the bill," and Leilani said, "Ok, I'll be back tomorrow," and left. She went back to the main lobby and told her family she would take Art home tomorrow. She told them not to worry; she can come back tomorrow to get him and bring him home. Hank raised his eyebrow as he looked at her semi disapproving, and she held his hand and urged him to please understand. They asked her if she were sure, and she said, "Yes, I think it would be good if just the two of us are on that long car ride home. He doesn't know any of you, and I don't want him to feel in any way uncomfortable", and they all understood. She returned to Art's room and told him she would be back tomorrow to take him home, and he said ok. They hugged each other, and she left.

The ride home was eerily quiet, and with so much to consider, Leilani's mind is racing. She finally met Hank, a great guy that she loves. She is having twins with him and wants to be his wife and build a family, but on the other hand, she already has a beautiful two-year-old daughter with Art. The last thing she wants to do is hurt either one of them. She wants to believe in her heart of hearts that Art will understand and accept whatever happens, and of course, he would be able to see Arabella whenever he wants. As sensitive as this situation is, she truly hopes everything will go well, and she also hopes that everyone will be happy. When they made it to Vegas, Leilani excused herself and told Hank she wants to get new clothes for Art because she is sure he doesn't have anything nice to wear for the long ride home, and he understood and left. She went to the mall and bought him some comfortable jogging suits, underwear, shoes, socks, body wash, deodorant, lotion, and Creed, his favorite cologne. She wanted him to be as comfortable as he possibly could.

Now knowing the whole story, Charles must get with Veronica to tell her what's going on. He calls her, and of course, it went to voicemail, so he sent her a text telling her Art is still alive, and Leilani is picking him up from Utah tomorrow, so the plans have changed. When Veronica read that text, her heart skipped a beat, and now she is- nervous. She immediately called Charles in a panic, asking him a million and one questions. He just told her the basics, that Art suffered injuries from the crash, was in the hospital for a while, and then went to rehab for recovery, but he is fine now and will be home tomorrow, and she broke down and cried. Veronica will now have to face Art and deal with the truth, which she never thought she would ever have to do. She replayed everything she has done over and over in her head and tried hard to think of something convincing that he would accept and hopefully forgive her. The problem is the truth is so inevitably horrible she's not sure he ever will forgive her for what she's done.

Charles told Veronica it's not just about Art forgiving her. Her biggest challenge right now is they collected-millions of-dollars that may need to be paid back. She needs to figure out how she's going to come up with all that money. Veronica doesn't realize that although she depleted most of her four million dollars, Leilani didn't so she could quickly return what she received. She asked Charles how Art was and is he ok. He told her he didn't see him, but Leilani is bringing him home tomorrow. She is a bundle of nerves, now feeling bad about getting rid of his things, including the two Westies. He will have to start his life over, but she could not have predicted this, so she is hoping he will understand.

In the morning, Leilani is ready to take the drive back to Utah, and she loads her car with an overnight bag with the clothes she bought for Art and places Arabella in her car seat in the back. She didn't tell him about Arabella because she wants him to meet his daughter in person. Feeling somber on the way back to Utah, her heart feels no longer broken. She sings songs with Arabella to keep her morale up because deep down inside, she is excited. Arabella is meeting her father for the very first time, and she looks like a princess. She has long, silky locs of curls and beautiful blue eyes, with full, dark lashes. She could not be more perfect, and Leilani knows he will fall in love the moment he lays eyes on her. Arabella has on her best outfit and smells heavenly. She believes having Arabella should make for a more enriched life because he must be depressed about losing his only son Philippe. Arabella looks exactly like Art, but Leilani wonders if he will see it or not.

When she arrived at the facility, the administrator had lots of documents for her to sign, but before she does, Leilani went to Art's room to give him the bag with his clothes and toiletries. The second they walked into his room, his eyes immediately shifted down towards Arabella. He looked at her, and for a few seconds, he was speechless but said, who do we have here? Staring at her intently, Leilani told him, "This is Arabella Love Graziani, your daughter."

In shock, Art immediately bursts into tears, and he reached down to pick her up, and she let him. Art hugged her with every ounce of his soul, and Leilani is touched. He said, "I had no idea. I think if I had known

112

about this beautiful little one, I probably would've made it home faster. How old is she? When was she born?" "She's two, born February fourteenth." "Wow, Art said, a Valentine baby." "Yes, Leilani said, that's why her middle name is Love. We call her BellaLove." "Bella Love Art said you are a real beauty, my little Princess." Leilani handed him the garment bag saying, "Here I thought you might like to put this on, so you will be comfortable for the ride home." "Yes, he said thank you so much; I appreciate this." "Listen, I need to go to the office to sign a bunch of papers and pay the bill. You get dressed, and we'll be right back." Ok, he said. She and Arabella left the room while he got ready, and she returned to the office to take care of the bill. Once he was ready, the three of them left the facility.

When they got to the car, Leilani suggested that Art sit in the back with Arabella to get better acquainted. They all sang songs together, and Art counts numbers go through the alphabet and name colors with Arabella. She is receptive to him, maybe because she can feel she belongs to him. Having the same eyes must make her feel at ease because she is the mirror image of him and never was there a dull moment with the two of them in the back seat. After about two hours, she fell asleep, and Art began to ask questions. Low and behold, he asked about Veronica, and Leilani was honest and said she hasn't talked to her since the accident. She is glad to know that he remembers her, thinking it must be a good sign, but at the same time, just hearing her name hits a sore spot. Art starts to reminisce and tells her he remembers the only time the two of them made love in Australia, saying, "Wow, I guess it was meant to be. Look at this beautiful little girl." "Yes, Leilani said, I love her life. She is a sweet and loving child, and you will love being around her," Leilani said with pride. Art watches her sleeping in the car seat next to him so peacefully, and he can't take his eyes off her.

Arriving in Vegas, Art looks around and noticeably sees the growth and build up over the time he's been away. He notices the route Leilani is taking, and he doesn't remember his house being in the direction she is driving, so he asks where they were going. "Oh, Leilani said, we're going to my place." "Your place? Art asked. Do you mean that little studio apartment?" "No Art, I bought a home after getting the money from your insurance company. Everyone thought you passed away in that plane crash." "But I left everything to you, so why didn't you just stay in my house"? "No, Art, you left everything to Veronica and gave me a hundred thousand dollars. I did think that was a bit strange, but who am I to tell you what to do with your money"? "What? Art shouted! That's total bullshit! It was just the opposite!" Shocked to hear what he just said, Leilani asked him to lower his voice and calm down, so he won't wake Arabella. Wow, Leilani thought, this is a new revelation.

"Listen, Art, let's not talk about that right now; we're almost at my house. Let's go inside and talk," as she pulled up to her house. Art looks all around and compliments her on the house. "Thank you; I appreciate that. It's my first house, and I'm kinda proud of it. You inspired me quite a bit with yours". Art smiled and said, "And speaking of my house, is Veronica living in it"? Leilani sighed and took a deep breath. "I have no idea, but Charles is dating my cousin Giselle." "Wow, really?" "Yes, really, and they seem to be happy." As they walked inside the house, Art is impressed. Her home is much smaller than his, but it's still a lovely house. It's decorated modern Boho, very clean and sleek, with many different colors and textures. She showed him all around and directed him into one of the guest rooms. Feeling disturbed about him saying he left her everything and not Veronica, she's wondering how it could've possibly happened the way that it did. Dismissing it for now, they have plenty of time to talk about that later. She grabs his arm and takes him into the kitchen to make him something to eat.

While she prepares the food, they catch up on everything else that has happened, and he listens intently. Anxious about Veronica, he brings it up again, but Leilani insists they should take care of that tomorrow, and for now, they need to enjoy the quiet time to catch up. Furious but trying not to let it show, Art says ok, and Leilani changes the subject. The three of them eat the food and enjoy the day. Leilani gets a few text messages from Hank, and she replies, *I love you, babe; I'll see you tomorrow.* Now Leilani feels it's time to explain her current situation.

She starts by saying they all thought he didn't make it from the plane crash because the charter jet company said there were no survivors. Finally, after a year and after Arabella's birth, she managed to move on with her life. She went on to explain just a little over a year ago; she met a wonderful man. They are about to be married and have twin girls on the way. Art said, "I wondered what was going on with your mid-area, but I didn't want to assume anything. Congratulations Lani, you deserve it."

Relieved that he isn't upset, she said, "Art, you would like him; he's a great guy." "Do you love him; does he treat you like a queen"? "Yes, I do, and yes, he does Art. He helped me get through a very dark place. He loves both me and Arabella. He stepped up to be a father to her, and I love him for that". "Ok, so, it's settled then, I will walk you down the aisle, I love you." "Thank you, Art. That's very sweet of you. I love you too, I'm so glad you're here."

"Now, moving on, let's discuss this issue with Veronica." Leilani dreads that Art keeps bringing her up, but she wants it resolved because it's a big deal. As Art goes on to ask more detailed questions, Leilani stops him and says, "Let me give you the readers digest version." She took a deep breath and said, "Ok, here goes. Right after the authorities signed off on your death, we all went to New York to see Tom and went over your trust, and the next day Veronica gave me a plane ticket back to Vegas and an eviction notice to have me removed from your house. Art interjected and said, "So she kicked you out just like that"? "Yes, because your trust designated one hundred thousand dollars for me, and everything else went to Veronica." Art put both his hands up to his face and took a deep breath as his heart began to crush and ache. As his thoughts raced back and forth, he sat there quiet for a moment, thinking about what he should do.

Leilani touched his arm and said, "look, Art, it's ok, the insurance company gave me four million dollars, and I haven't even touched it; besides, you're here now, so everything is ok." Art said in a stern tone, "No, Leilani, you don't understand; if she's been in that house this whole time,

I'm sure she helped herself to my cash I've kept in the safe!" "Oh, Leilani said, I didn't know you kept cash in a safe. How much did you keep in there"? Art looked at her and said, "millions." Leilani replied, "But look, she got millions too, so maybe she didn't touch it." "Well, for her sake, I hope you're right because that insurance money might need to be paid back, or at least what you two received for me. Either way, I'm going to find out first thing tomorrow when I go over there. It will be a long night for me, but I know I need to be calm when speaking to her. Right now, I'm just so angry." "Right, I get it. Do you want me to take you over there?" "No, sweetie, I'll take a taxi, but thanks anyway." She said ok and handed him a few hundred dollars. "Here she said, you need some money in your pocket."

Art woke up early the next morning, showered, called a taxi, and got dressed. His taxi arrived shortly after, and he got out of the house just before Leilani woke up. He headed right over to his house and could not wait to confront Veronica. When Art arrived at his home, he sat in the taxi for just a moment to take it all in, then paid the fare and tipped the driver. He walked up to the door and rang the bell. It took two rings until Veronica answered, and when she opened the door, they both were surprised at the sight of each other. Art lost a lot of weight, had a buzz haircut, and Veronica looked like she aged ten years. Her hair is cut short in a pixie style, and her eyes were very swollen like she had been crying. She immediately reached out and hugged him, and awkwardly offered for him to come inside.

As Art walked inside, he was relieved to see that his house still looked the same for the most part. She offered him a seat and made him a cup of coffee. Right away, Art explained to her that this must be such a shock but moving forward, the two of them have some serious talking to do. She looked at him with sad, puppy dog eyes and said she understood. Before he sat down, he immediately walked into his office to check the safe. Veronica followed him, and before he could even open it, she said, "Art, it's all gone, nothing is in there, I'm sorry." Enraged, he slammed his fist on the wall and shouted, "Why Veronica, why? Now crying profusely, she pleaded with him not to be angry, but that ship has already sailed. She urged him to please let her explain. He furiously looked at her and caught himself and said to her, "So tell me how you plan on fixing this, Veronica. I know how much money I had in that safe!" She asked him just to have a seat so they can talk rationally.

She went on to explain that she spent quite a bit of money getting the Colorado farm up and running, how she had breast cancer, paying a surrogate, ultimately losing her baby, and having to pay for it all. He allowed her to explain how she could use the profits to pay him back and how sorry she was. He listened to her every word, and when she finished, he asked her, "But what about the insurance money? Leilani still has her portion and is prepared to pay it back right now. How do you plan on paying the money back, Veronica?" She explained that she couldn't produce millions of dollars immediately because she gave that money to her foster dad to invest in more gas stations in Ohio.

Of course, she left out the part about giving Tom the one million dollars, but Art asked how the trust got changed? Instead of confessing about the million, she told him she just had the docs changed. Then he asked her why. "Art, I helped you in so many ways to make some of the money you've made, and I just felt so insulted that you thought so little of me by only giving me a hundred thousand dollars and giving everything else to Leilani. I was shocked when I saw that. Now I understand that was just a trust, and maybe you were planning on modifying it later, but when you were suddenly pronounced dead, I could not see things going that way. Look, I know I was wrong, but I will do everything I can to fix this Art. Please give me a chance."

Art looked at Veronica for a moment and said, "You're right; you are going to fix this because I am pissed"! She pleaded with him to give her the chance to fix it, then he asked about Charles. Sadly, she told him they broke up not long after the baby died, and Art expressed his sadness about her having cancer and gave his condolences about the baby. She did her best to convince him that she can fix it, and he looked at her and said he's not so sure, but he is willing to give her a chance. He looked out the window toward the backyard where the guesthouse and garages were and asked what happened. She explained the Tennent fire, destroying both the guest house, the garage, and the cars, and he just shook his head. Veronica said, "But hey, now that you're here alive and well, the insurance company should fix everything from the fire and make you whole again, right?" Art said, "I don't know, but I will find out."

Sensing that Art seems to be calmer and possibly open to forgiving her, she asks if it's ok for her to stay at the house until she can get a place of her own, and he said, ok for now. He could never kick her out as she did to Leilani. She hands him an itemized spreadsheet accounting of everything, showing him how she made sure everything regarding all his properties stayed current. He thanks her and said, let's just get all this fixed. Relieved that Art isn't as angry as she thought he would be, she asks if Leilani hates her, and he told her, "Leilani doesn't hate anyone. She is living her best life right now, so don't worry about her. Then Art asks, what about all my things? What did you do with them?" Veronica told him she donated his clothes and shoes to a consignment shop. He replied by saying, "That's ok; I can always get new clothes. I've lost so much weight they probably wouldn't have fit me anyway", and Veronica quickly agreed. "Ok, Art said, Let's go shopping. You have money, right?" "Yes, of course, Veronica said, let's go."

Art and Veronica talked and shopped for most of the day, and she congratulated him on Arabella. Art replied, "Oh, so you know about her?" "Yes, she said; Charles showed me a picture of her. She's beautiful; I can't get over how much she looks like you." "Yes, Art said, smiling; she does, doesn't she? I just feel so blessed to have her in my life. I was depressed for a long time about losing Philippe. I brought him here to this country from France, and he did not deserve to die. I feel so guilty and had so many plans for him, and now he's gone. My heart aches for him, but Arabella gives me a new look at life. She is a jewel, and I will make sure she has a beautiful life, no matter what it takes." Veronica watched Art as he spoke about his

120

little girl, and it made her want to cry. She may never have another child, and her heart feels like it's broken beyond repair.

Meanwhile, Leilani, Giselle, and Tony are at her house, talking about everything that has happened. Giselle puts her two cents in and asks Leilani how she feels about what Veronica did to her. Leilani replies, "Whatever Art decides to do is fine. I'm just happy that he is here to be in Arabella's life." Then Charles rings the bell and joins them. Giselle is glad to see him. Tony calls Isabella to come over, and Leilani sends Hank a text to stop by.

Tony and Leilani whip up something tasty for everyone to eat as Hank, Isabella, and Gabriella also arrive. Leilani takes Gabi upstairs to hang out with Arabella and the sitter. The adults all talk, listen to music and eat while the guys play pool, like usual. The ladies move into the next room away from the guys and make plans to help Leilani with the wedding, and she tells them that Art will walk her down the aisle, and thinking about having the wedding at his house. Art's home is beautiful, and his backyard is four times the size of hers, making it the perfect place for a wedding. Giselle asks, "Are you sure Hank will be ok with that?" Leilani said, "I don't know, but we're all going to have to coexist and co-parent together, so we might as well start now. I will talk with Hank, don't worry."

They all went to their rooms to hang out and chill. Giselle turned on some soft music and finally told him she's pregnant. Shocked and surprised, he picks her up and hugs her tight. Elated about being a dad again after losing his baby girl Alayna, he feels close to Giselle and loves her now more than ever. They made sweet, passionate love until the wee hours of the morning until they fell asleep.

Chapter Seven

Celebrating More Family Blending

It's just before midnight, and Hank kisses Leilani on her forehead as she reaches ten centimeters delivering their beautiful baby girls, Issa Eleni and Kaira Aster, both healthy weighing in at just over five pounds each. Her labor lasted nine hours, and she is exhausted but overjoyed with love for her two beautiful new babies. The nursery at the house is ready for their homecoming, and Leilani hired a nurse to help. Months before, the wedding planner, Leilani, Giselle, and Isabella, made all the arrangements for the wedding, so all Leilani needs to do is recover from giving birth to those beautiful twin baby girls. The date is set, and Hank is ok with having the wedding and reception at Art's house. Hank's twin sisters arrive a week before the wedding because they want to help with the babies. Hank is flying his parents out, and Leilani will fly two of her aunts and uncles and a few cousins out the weekend of the wedding and put them all up at the Wynn.

Giselle moved in with Charles, so they can be together when their baby is born. Shortly after the arrival of Leilani and Hanks twins, their beautiful baby girl was born as well. She is gorgeous, and they named her after their mothers, Mina and Corrine. Now both Leilani and Giselle have newborns, and they love every minute of them. The first-night family arrived, Tony prepares a feast at the house so everyone could get acquainted, including Art. The Bourdeau's, Leilani's family, loved Hank, Charles, Isabella, and Gabriella, and the Tesfaye's Hanks' family loved everyone as well. Everyone was excited about the wedding and all the beautiful babies. Happy times shared of great food, music, laughing, talking, dancing, and moments of bliss from this newly blended family are all captured by the videographer crew that Leilani hired for the wedding.

Veronica still has quite a bit on her plate, trying to make things right with Art, and she doesn't want to do anything to put him on edge, considering what's at stake. Still living in his house, Art urges her to try and make things right with Leilani. Since her wedding will be at his home, sooner than later would be the perfect time to make amends, and Veronica agreed. The wedding planner transformed Arts backyard into a magical wonderland. A fully air-conditioned, fully enclosed tent is set up even though the weather is nice. Beautiful and fragrant flowers are throughout this glamourous space with their favorite music playing. At the top of the tent are several brilliant chandeliers, and lit candles are on every table. Bar and dessert stations are on both sides of the room. Everything is breathtakingly beautiful and is sure to amaze and delight each guest.

Just a few hours before the ceremony, Leilani and Giselle are upstairs in one of Art's spare rooms, getting ready with their babies in tow. The videographer is also there, capturing some of the first moments of the day. Veronica's room is just down the hall, so she knocked on the door to see if Leilani is willing to speak with her. Giselle opens the door and lets her in, not realizing who she is. As Veronica walks in, she immediately sees the three beautiful babies sleeping, and on her left, looking like a porcelain doll, is Arabella sitting in a chair. She pauses for a second, looking at the beauty of these children, and then as she looks further into the room, Leilani is getting her face beat from Makeup by Belkis.

Once they make eye contact, Veronica apologizes for the intrusion and tells Leilani how beautiful she looks. Veronica felt speechless from looking at those babies, plus not knowing who Giselle is; she offered Leilani congratulations, bid her a good day, and left. Giselle had never met Veronica. She asked Leilani who she was. "That was Veronica." Giselle was so upset, she wanted to fight Veronica, but Leilani calmed her down and told her not to worry about her. Today is her wedding, and she doesn't want anything to ruin her day.

As guests begin to arrive, Art walks in and passes by Veronica, catching her off guard, and startles her. Their eyes meet as she gives him a nod, then he asked her if she got the chance to see Leilani. She quickly said yes, and he gave her a cheerful wink and a thumbs-up, and she nervously smiled. He is in a great mood and is very pleased with how everything looks. As Veronica gazes at all the guests arriving, she guesstimates who Leilani's family members are and who are the grooms. She sees Charles standing with a very handsome dark gentleman who she believes is the groom. He and Hank are quietly chopping it up. Throwing his head back laughing, Charles spots Veronica and immediately stops laughing.

She walked over to him to say hello, and he introduced her to Hank. She congratulated him and gave Charles a pathetic hug. When she walked away, Hank said, "Oh, so that's your old girl"? Charles said, "Yeah, I'm surprised she's even here," grabbing his phone to text Giselle asking her if Leilani knew Veronica was here, and she replied, "yes, it's all good."

As the ceremony begins, Arabella walked down the aisle throwing flower petals up in the air above her head, watching them fall all around her like snowflakes. Hanks' twin sisters walked in just ten steps behind, each holding his now fully awake twin daughters wrapped in a silky, floral blanket. The guests gasped with joy as the bridal party walked to the music's beat down the aisle and then circling Hank to the music's rhythm. Next, Tony and Isabella walked in. Then, Giselle walked in with Charles and joining the circle around Hank as they all throw rose petals up, falling on him, delighting the guests even more. Once they are standing next to Hank, the music changes. Everyone stood up as Art walked in arm and arm with Leilani and all eyes were on her. She is astonishingly gorgeous as she focuses directly on Hank, and he focuses on her. With Charles carrying the ring in his pocket, he handed it to Hank. The minister starts the ceremony, and the two recite their vows. Hank slips the ring on her finger; they are pronounced man and wife, kiss each other passionately, and the crowd cheered.

The reception immediately began, and everyone started socializing and interacting with the bride and groom. Veronica walked the room and tried to stay unseen but did notice Charles sitting with Giselle. She watched them for a while, and to her, they looked like a couple. After everyone ate dinner, a lady walked over to them, holding one of the babies she saw in the room earlier, and hands her to Charles. Devastated watching them dote over her, Veronica could see the baby must belong to the two of them, and her heart feels crushed. Leilani has Art's beautiful three-year-old daughter, plus she has those gorgeous twins, and Veronica has no one and nothing. As she looks over to the right, she spots Art conversing with people doting over Arabella. The entire room is cheerful and happy about the nuptials, and the babies just made her want to leave. She just wants to die watching everything going on, and she had no idea Charles was going to be a part of all this. Witnessing all this wedding bliss lets her know that she clearly must move on.

The next day, the newlyweds jet off to Santorini, Greece, for a seven-day honeymoon, and their three daughters stay behind with the Nanny and the sitter. They booked a gorgeous Caldera suite at the Iconic Luxury Boutique Hotel and walking in felt like they stepped into a close Greek friends' home. Their suite included five-star amenities, including a private jetted plunge pool on their balcony. That night the couple consummated their blissful marriage under the starlit skies of Greece. On day two, they took a private guided street tour to explore the entire island at their own pace. The next day, they booked a private catamaran to enjoy the island's best beaches and magnificent views. Each day, they enjoyed incredible Greek cuisine at the best restaurants and were by far better than anything they ever ate in the states. Every morning they had breakfast on their balcony overlooking the panoramic Cyclades architecture of the southern Aegean Sea. They passionately made love every night, enjoying the spectacular golden and fuchsia sunsets. They shopped in Fira for gifts and souvenirs to take home to their families on their last two days. The whole atmosphere of this trip left them feeling recharged and more in love, promising each other that they will return someday.

Returning home from the eighteen-hour flight felt surreal and somewhat draining, but they made it home safe and were glad to be back with their babies. Hank took an extra day off work to move most of his personal belongings to Leilani's house because hers is bigger and more accommodating. Not quite ready to go home, his twin sisters Zara and Zoe are still in Vegas at his place. As Hank packs his things, he chats with them, and they tell him they want to stay. They've searched for jobs and have interviews set up. Although he is surprised, he said ok and told them they could continue staying at his house until it sells since he and Leilani plan to buy a house together. Elated that he approves, they promise to help babysit anytime they want. Hank told them that if they get a job, he will make sure they have a reliable car to get around in. He suggests they could work at Leilani's center if they wanted and said ok, so he made the call, and Leilani said yes and to be there tomorrow at 10:00 am, and they are excited.

The next morning Hanks twin sisters, Zara and Zoe, arrived at the center-right on time. The daycare manager spoke with them and showed them around the facility. Since the girls are good with children, Leilani thought the daycare would be the right place for them to start. They take the job and are happy about being able to stay in Vegas. Meanwhile, Art and

Veronica met up to discuss what she plans to do about getting that money back to the Insurance company. As she explained to Art, she no longer has the money and hoped she could pay it back with the cannabis farm's profits. Art immediately interjected and said, "That's not going to work for me." He told her he needs more information about the gas stations that her foster dad has. He reminded her she could go to jail for what she did. He also told her she's lucky Leilani has a good heart because she probably would be in prison by now if it were anyone else. He reminded her again that Leilani still has her portion of that money and is prepared to give it back whenever necessary. Hearing that made Veronica cringe with anger, but she tried not to let it show. With Veronica not speaking up fast enough, Art said, "Let's take a trip out to Cleveland, so I can see these gas stations and talk with your dad face to face," and all Veronica could say was ok.

Veronica contacted the charter jet company that houses Art's jet to reserve a flight out to Cleveland, and they flew out. On the plane, Art asked her to explain the investment. She told him the cost was $1.9 million per station with an annual cost of $250,000 to operate, plus $160,000 annually to buy stock products, which usually profits around $300,000 a year, roughly $25k a month, and starting next month, her dad will send her $20k a month. Art said, "So your dad will keep $5k every month?" "Yes, because since she's not able to be there to run them, he will, and she thinks him only keeping $5K a month to make sure both stations run correctly is worth it."

So now, Art tells her how things are going to go. He will get the $20K every month, even though that's less than a quarter of a million dollars a year. Next, he told her their profit split for the farm would change from sixty/forty to her only getting ten percent, which allows her to repay the money she owes faster. She should end up with about seven to nine thousand dollars a month, which is enough for her living expenses. If she hadn't been driven by greed, taking everything from Leilani, she could've had a good life getting forty percent of the cannabis farm profits. Now she's back where she started, except she no longer has Art's trust and support.

They arrived in Cleveland late in the evening, and Art booked two rooms at the Holiday Inn. They are meeting with her foster dad first thing in the morning, so they went to sleep to start fresh in the morning. Art has the documents and is fully expecting her dad to agree to the terms and sign it, and then they can fly back home that same day. Veronica already explained everything to her dad about what the alternative would be for her, hoping it will be quick and painless. It's hard for her to fall asleep because too many thoughts are going through her head. Feeling embarrassed, her foster dad thought she hit the jackpot, getting all that money, and now she feels ashamed that her circumstances have changed. They met her dad at his office, and Art is impressed with everything. It's a modern office with a lobby and several offices in the back, including two rooms set up with surveillance monitors for all six of his stations. Each room has twelve monitors with two employees in each room watching every angle of his stations, inside and out.

Both men agree that it's unfortunate that they are meeting under those regrettable circumstances, but the bottom line is having to do this was inevitable. Art is not interested in owning gas stations in Ohio, so getting the revenue of twenty thousand dollars every month is just fine with him. Veronica's foster dad is ok with only getting the five thousand every month because that's all he was getting in the first place. Art only wants his money back, so when it's all paid, she and her dad will own the stations outright, and he doesn't care. Art's agreement is ironclad and non-negotiable, so Veronica's foster dad just signed it. The two men shake hands, thanked each other, and Art turned to leave. Veronica wanted to speak with her foster dad, so she asked Art to give her a minute to talk to him, and he said, of course. Her foster dad said to Veronica, "Art came out here just for me to sign that agreement? He could've done that through the mail". "No, Veronica replied, "he needs to look you in the eye. Anytime Art conducts any business; he likes to do it face to face. He wants to study you and keep who you are in his head, so he won't forget you if something falls short or goes wrong with the payments. He's from New York and has an old school way of thinking and doing things".

On the flight home, Veronica asked Art about Charles' new life and baby. Sensing her despair, he put it to her delicately just by saying, he is happy, he has moved on, and you should do the same." He also told her the circle is growing with beautiful people, and if she does the right thing, she could come back into it. Feeling like such an outsider, what Art said is comforting, and she is heavily considering it. If not, she just may move to Colorado to start a new life. Right now, as painful as it is to see Charles obviously in love with someone else, plus having a new baby is too difficult for her to watch. Time will tell and if she's ever going to be comfortable with them remains to be seen.

Tony and Isabella are doing well with their relationship and are falling deeper in love. Her thirtieth birthday is coming up, so he wants to give her a party at the house. Having family and friends over is one of Leilani's favorite things to do, so of course, she and Hank said yes. Excited about having another party, Giselle, Zara, Zoe, and Leilani go into party mode and start planning it. Since it's Isabella's thirtieth birthday, they want Isabella to feel special, so they go all out with the plans. About thirty of Isabella's closest friends and family came out, and Leilani's usual crowd attended the party as well. Tony hired an authentic Puerto Rican caterer to prepare Isabella's favorites like; Tostones with Sofrito salsa, Mofongo, Arroz con Pollo, crispy Pastelon de amarillos, Pastelillos de Carne, Pernil, and shrimp Camarones Guisados, just to name a few. The caterer did an excellent job with the food, and everything turned out amazing, and all the guests loved it. Leilani had her Nanny and four girls from the centers' daycare to care for all the kids.

As Isabella's guests arrive, Art came with Veronica and is in heaven, meeting Isabella's female friends that are each prettier than the next. Looking at those sexy, gorgeous ladies made him feel like a kid in a candy store, so he works the room, and Veronica does the same as there are several attractive men there as well. Veronica sets her bottle of wine on the counter, looks all around Leilani's house, and is impressed. As Art makes his way around the house, he spots Sofia. He is instantly mesmerized at the sight of her stunning beauty. As he makes his way over to her, he doesn't see anyone else in the room. Every inch of her is perfect; she is tall with a barbie doll figure, beautiful, fire-red hair, a flawless smile, and big, brown cat eyes, looking just like the Columbian actress Sofia Vegara. Art introduced himself, and she answered with that heavy Columbian accent just like the actress, which Art thought was sexy as hell. They engaged in pleasantries, and every time Art made her laugh, she kept touching his arms and shoulders, which turned him on. They are obviously attracted to each other, and when Art whispered in her ear, he kissed her neck, and she turned around and kissed his lips. With the alcohol kicking in, they both continue their touchy-feely antics until their touches became more intimate, as they got better acquainted. Before they got too far, they were asked to join everyone in a friendly word and action game.

The game they played was fun, but it calls for partners, allowing everyone to feel more comfortable with each other, and Veronica attempts to go for it and join in. She is broken-hearted but still a beautiful woman, especially to someone who doesn't know her sad past. She has her eyes on a man who looks like the CSI actor Adam Rodriguez. Julio noticed Veronica as well, so he approaches her to partner up, and he strikes up a conversation with her. Veronica finds him quite handsome and charming, but she can see he is a little shy, so she attempts to make him feel at ease by saying she won't bite him unless he wants her to. Laughing, he let his guard down, and the two continue to chat. Isabella is his cousin, and Veronica just said she's Art and Leilani's friend. "Cool, he said; Leilani and Hank seem to be cool people, having this party for my cousin at their house and all. My

133

cousin seems to be happy with her man Tony. I like him; he's a cool dude. Just as long as he doesn't hurt her, he's cool with me". Veronica replied," Oh, so you're the protective type, huh?". "Yep, you can say that."

As they all continue to play the game, the intimate questions get deeper and deeper. Even though the alcohol takes effect, the challenges always get everyone's attention. Sofia's challenge is to do a show and tell of kissing someone, and she chose to kiss Art. She explained and demonstrated how she would kiss him every day and every night if he were her man. The way Sofia kissed Art made him want to take her home right then and there and never let her go. He is attracted to her, and she keeps turning him on by the minute. She is such a gorgeous woman, he feels like he hit the jackpot, but did he really, or did she?

Sofia grew up in the Bronx and is a first cousin to Isabella. Their dads are brothers from Columbia, and the two women are very close. Sofia's mom is also Columbian like her dad, but Isabella's mom is Puerto Rican from San Juan. Sofia's parents had six kids, so making ends meet often left them with very little. She didn't attend college; she had to get a job to help support the family because she is the oldest. An excellent typist and a natural in office settings, she has impeccable secretarial skills, plus being bi-lingual gives her that extra edge in the workforce. Art doesn't care what she does for a living because she won't be doing it much longer if he has it his way. Sofia's beauty intimidates most guys, so she is often overlooked, but Art doesn't scare easily. She has the qualities any man would want in a woman and then some, so he pursues her relentlessly without hesitation.

After the game, the caterer brought out sliced pieces of birthday cake for everyone to enjoy. As everyone nibbles on the cake, Tony gets on one knee, professes his love for Isabella, and asks for her hand in marriage. Shocked and surprised, she says yes, and everyone stopped eating their cake and cheered them on. It looks like another wedding is on the way, and Leilani couldn't be happier for the two of them. Charles looks at Giselle and says, we're next, babe. The guests brought Isabella lots of birthday gifts, and she meticulously opened each one as everyone oohed and awed. By the end of the night, Art and Sofia look more like a couple as his charm fully captivates her undivided attention. He is smitten and offers to take her home, and she accepts. As the two of them attempt to leave quietly, it doesn't go unnoticed by Veronica. She doesn't want to stay there without Art, but she is engaging with Julio, so she decided to stay. Art and Sofia snuck out together, and he forgot all about Veronica.

As Art escorted Sofia to his brand-new Bentley that he purchased through Charles the day before, she melts into the plush seat loving all its luxuriousness. She's never been in such a high-end car like this before, so she takes it all in. Feeling like Cinderella, her heart starts to flutter, wondering how rich Art must be having a car like that. Once he got inside, she started giving him directions to her house, but he interjects and asks if she'd like to go to his house instead, and she said yes. When they arrive at Art's home, he turns on his surround sound, playing soft romantic music, and pours drinks as Sofia looks around sheepishly. He invited her to get comfortable and make herself at home. She can see his house is massive and wonders if he lives alone. Sensing her curiosity, he told her his former assistant Veronica lives there until she gets a place of her own, and his housekeeper Maria has been there for years.

He gently took her hand and showed her each room and the backyard. Art's custom home is beautifully furnished and has all the top of the line furnishings. Sofia has never been in a house of this magnitude, so initially, she is nervous, but he quickly made her feel like she belongs there. They talk for a couple of hours, and Art asks Sofia about her goals and dreams in life. When she told him her main goal in life was to be happy regardless of what she does for a living, he knew he wanted to be a part of that happiness.

They share many personal stories of growing up in New York, even though their experiences were as opposite as day and night. His upbringing on the upper east side was very privileged, and hers was very meager in the south Bronx. Either way, they consider themselves as New Yorkers at heart and have similar mindsets about what they want in life now. The more they talk, the more attracted he is to her, so he invites her to take a New York trip for a few days, and she accepted. He wants to make love to her this instant, but he decides to wait because he doesn't want to come on too strong with her. They continue to make out and talk about things they like to do, and finally, he asks if she's ready to go home. She told him that she could stay there with him forever, and he told her she could if she wanted to. Laughing, Sofia said she's serious, and he said so was he. Art is a good guy, and even though he's been through hell and back, he is still very financially stable, so all he wants now is to be happy. Sofia is gorgeous and wants to be happy as well. Their chance meeting at the birthday party is the beginning of her fairytale life. He took her home just before sunrise, and she felt like Cinderella going home from the ball after meeting her Prince Charming.

As soon as she got inside her house, she immediately went to her bedroom and called Isabella to tell her about Art. She told her what they did the night before and asked her to go to New York with him for a few days. Isabella was happy and told her based on everything Tony told her about him, Art is a good guy and is financially set, so she doesn't have to worry about him being a creep or anything. She told her to have fun and gave her the green light. Delighted to get her cousin's approval, she packed for their trip. Art had Veronica drive them to the airport, and she remained quiet during the ride as Art and Sofia sat in the back.

When they pulled into the private side of McCarran, Sofia was surprised that they were flying private. It's the beginning of another glimpse of Art's opulent lifestyle. Being on a private plane was also the first time for Sofia, but again she is delighted and takes it all in. The flight attendant and pilot extend a warm welcome to them as they board the jet. In the cabin, she is delighted to see two dozen red roses on her seat. She picked them up to smell them, and of course, they smelled amazing, and she turned around to hug and kiss him. Surrounded by all this luxury makes her feel special, and precisely how Art wanted her to feel. Once the door closes and takes flight, the flight attendant opens a champagne bottle, pours them a glass, and serves them a tasty meal.

As they land at New Haven airport, a waiting car picks them up, drives them to Montauk, and arrives at his beautiful Hamptons home that Veronica redecorated. Now Sofia is thinking everything just keeps getting better and better as she looks at all the grandeur of his other home. He had the kitchen well stocked with her favorite things to eat and drink, which Sofia felt was very thoughtful and attentive. He showed her around and directed her to the master bedroom so she can freshen up and unpack. Just like Veronica always planned in the past, Art had a private Chef prepare their first meal at the house as they sat out back to watch the sunset and take in the beautiful sounds of the water. Sofia is so relaxed and comfortable with Art; it feels more like a dream than reality. She enjoys all the details he put into everything and is cool with hanging out and relaxing; however, he has plans for them in the morning. As the evening progresses, the two continue to talk, laugh, eat, dance, and drink. Eventually, they become a little tired and are ready to go to bed. As he alludes to turn in for the night in one of the other bedrooms, she invites him to join her in the Master bedroom, and he gladly accepts.

Their mutual attraction led them to Arts master bedroom's silky sheets overlooking the oceans' waves and starlit sky. He takes his time with Sofia and loves every bit of her flesh as they engulf each other's bodies. As he slowly tastes her sweet nectar, he devourers every drop, caressing and softly sucking on her clit until she floods the sheets. Grabbing his penis with only her mouth, she sucked it like no other woman has ever done to him before. She sucked him until he exploded, swallowing every ounce of his cum, and never took her eyes off his. He watched her take his full load and was impressed. Still hard, he had to enter her, and when he did, she squeezed her vaginal walls tightly on his hard penis as he stroked in and out, drawing him back in on every attempted exit.

With his mind blown, he keeps going and going, stroking faster and then slowly until they climax together and fall into each other's arms. Art likes their groove, and after a few minutes, they are both ready to do it all over again, but they went to a different room because the sheets are soaked. They slept in late the next morning, and after Art snacked on Sofia, they ate breakfast. Art ordered a limo to take them into the city early that evening for dinner at Carmines on 44th St. and then to the Minskoff theatre to see The Lion King. They enjoyed the dinner and the show, and just like two young lovers, they held hands and kissed during their ride back to Montauk.

Arriving back to Vegas, Art and Sofia saw the most popular shows and concerts on the strip over the next few months and continued to grow closer. Their relationship is now at the point where he doesn't want her to go home. She drives a bucket, so Art bought her a new Audi Q3 to get around town better, and she is delighted. He asks if she likes being with him, and of course, she said yes. Art asks her to marry him, she said yes, and they went ring shopping. He bought her an elegant seven-carat emerald cut diamond ring that she adores. Feeling much like a princess, she loves how he dotes over her and how he always makes her feel special. Next on their agenda is discussing the wedding and honeymoon. They both decide to have the wedding at Art's house, and for their honeymoon, they decided to go to the Island of the Gods in Bali for seven days. Art called Leilani to tell her he'd like to get together with everyone at his house on the weekend, and she said yes, of course.

The night of the get-together, everyone arrived promptly at eight o'clock, including Veronica. None of them knew the reason for the occasion, but any time there's a gathering at Art's house, everyone knows it's worth attending. Art had all the food catered in, and he ordered lots of flowers and booze. He had lots of delectable hors d'oeuvres, tasty appetizers, a dessert table, a full bar, and of course, music. Once all the guests are there, Art gets everyone's attention by saying he has an announcement. The loud chatter of conversations and laughter quickly came to a halt as Art stood up to speak. He thanked everyone for coming and announced that he and Sofia are getting married. They all stood up, cheered, and congratulated them with lots of hugs and kisses. Isabella, excited for the two of them, already knew their path, so she knew it was just a matter of time. Veronica, on the other hand, isn't so excited for obvious reasons.

Veronica once handled many things for Art, but now, the two aren't as close after what's happened. She realizes she screwed up and thought their decade long relationship could endure anything, and never in her wildest dreams did she think they would turn out like this. Either way, Art is about to have a wife soon, so Veronica knows it's time to move out of his house. Looking across the room, she spots Charles interacting with his woman Giselle doting over her, feeling displaced, being the only single person amongst the group. Looking to her left, recognizing a familiar face, seeing Isabella's cousin Julio offers relief. She hasn't seen him in a while, so she walked over to him to strike up a conversation. They didn't get very far when they first met, so she attempted to rekindle their acquaintance to see what happens.

He ingeniously engages with her as she does most of the talking. Despite their failure to make an encouraging connection the last time, he compliments her and says, "Hey, how are you? It's been a while." She surveys the crowd one more time and notices everyone is either coupled up or engaging in threes and fours, so she starts to feel out of place once again. The music is off the chain, and a slow jam comes on, so she takes his hand and starts dancing right where they stood, allowing him to be close so he can feel her toned body.

As Art and Sofia play around dancing provocatively, kissing and grinding on each other, the crowd starts laughing and cheering and shouting, get a room! The more Art and Sofia bump and grind, the more envious Veronica becomes, so she snuggled into Julio's arms and pressed her body onto his. Veronica's getting turned on because it's been a while since she's been in a man's arms. Veronica noticed all the slow jams playing are baby-making songs or songs about babies, then suddenly Sofia clanged her glass and said she has an announcement to make. Surprised and curious, everyone stopped what they were doing again. She thanked everyone for coming and professes how happy she's been since she met Art. She presented Art with a small gift-wrapped box. When he opened it, there was a positive pregnancy test stick inside. As his eyes widened with excitement feeling thrilled with love, he hugged and kissed her, and then he looked up, thanking God for the blessing. They all shouted congratulations, and everybody started hugging again! What a great night for Art as his beautiful circle of beloved friends gets bigger. Leilani looked at him from across the room, delighted to see him so happy; her heart melts. As their eyes met, she smiled, he smiled back, and he gave her a wink. She is truly happy for him, and the look on his face is priceless.

Since the wedding would be at Art's house, Leilani recommended her event planner for the occasion, and Art and Sofia agreed, and she handled everything quickly for them. Art spared no expense making this wedding an affair that Sofia will never forget. Beautifully put together, everything turned out perfect. The ceremony was quaint and emotional, and there wasn't a dry eye in the place. No surprise, Sofia was stunning in her designer couture wedding gown, and Art can't take his eyes off her. When he spoke about being lost and assumed dead for almost two years, thinking he would never get back to his real life, everyone cried. He courageously talked about losing his son Philippe, having his beautiful daughter Arabella, and now being blessed again with his lovely wife Sofia and their baby on the way. Love has come full circle for him, and with tears running down her face, Leilani can't help but wonder if they would've been the ones getting married had that tragic accident not happened. Hank leaned over and kissed her face as she appears to be deep in thought. She shakes her head and wipes away tears feeling blessed to have Arabella, Hank, and their two beautiful twin daughters Issa and Kaira.

Immediately after the reception, the newlyweds left for their honeymoon in Bali for the next seven days. Veronica doesn't think she is mentally strong enough to deal with another wedding or baby being born into this group. Her life these past two years in Vegas has been too depressing, so she's considering moving to Colorado to start a new life. Hesitant about moving, Veronica went there one more time to see if it's a good place to live. While waiting at the airport, from a distance, she sees Julio at the luggage check-in. Shocked, he appears to be with a wife and three kids. Damn, she thought, wanting to melt into her seat and not wanting to be seen; what a waste, maybe Colorado won't be so bad after all.

Thinking about messing with him a little, she pulled out her cell phone and called him to see if he would answer. As his phone rang, she watched him, but he didn't answer it, so then she sent him a text, and called again. She saw him nervously grabbing his phone, look at it, and shake his head. Then she saw his "wife" say something to him, and he just shook his head again. Veronica called him again, and at that point, he looked irritated, so she hung up. After watching him squirm, Veronica busted out laughing and called him again. She continued to play the juvenile antics because it was the only thing she could do to keep from crying, so she called him one more time just to see him sweat. Thinking to herself, thank goodness it's time for her to board the flight, game over. Looking fierce, she stood up and intentionally walked right by him, making sure he saw her, and the look on his face was so hilarious, she laughed out loud again. Once she got settled into her seat on the plane, her cell phone rang, and it was Julio. She sent him straight to voicemail and blocked him *cuz she ain't got time for that*. Rocky Mountain high, here she comes.

Chapter Eight

Live, Love, Laugh, and Travel

Art and Sofia are in Jimbaran's Gili islands, Bali celebrating their honeymoon and plan to be back in time for Charles and Giselle's wedding. They booked a suite at the Fox Hotel, a five-star resort that sits on a private beach. Their room has all the high-end accommodations and amenities, so they are pleased. This property has beautiful hardwood flooring throughout, full-width windows with spectacular views, and great dining choices. Sofia truly feels like a queen as Art dotes over her every step of the way.

The first activity they booked was a full-body couples spa, including manicures, pedicures, facials, and massages to unwind and feel relaxed. That evening they enjoyed a Polynesian feast at a nearby restaurant and watched the sunset before returning to their hotel. The next day, they started their journey at the Ayana resort to make custom perfumes at a workshop in L'Atelier Parfumes et Creations. They loved the scents they created and purchased lots of bottles to take home and give to family and friends.

The next day after breakfast, they walked along the beach for a little while and enjoyed the scenery and engaged with other couples along the way. That evening, they ate a delicious seafood BBQ at the hotel while the Tari Kecak fire dancers performed on the beach at sunset. Although their days were long, they always saved enough energy for multiple romantic sessions of honeymoon lovemaking. Art had the hotel staff fill their room with dozens of candles and several beautiful floral arrangements while watching the fire show and dinner, to Sofia's delight upon returning.

The following morning after eating breakfast in bed, they went into the city to shop at the Conventional market to explore and join in on the local life. They ate lunch and shopped more at the Badung and Kumbasari Night Market. They bought authentic, native clothing to feel comfortable and some nice souvenirs to take home. Throughout their days and nights, they took lots of selfies and are having a great time. The next night, they enjoyed a delicious dinner cruise on a yacht on the Indian ocean while watching the breathtaking orange sunset below the horizon and starlit sky. Their next day's activities included a submarine voyage exploring all the underwater world views of beautiful coral reefs and colorful fish. Another honeymooning couple told them about the Bali Safari and marine park, so they went there to see the beautiful and majestic lions, white tigers, and bears later that day. On their final night, they stayed at the hotel, relaxed and packed. For them, making love in this region of the world was a honeymoon of their dreams and will be forever cherished in their hearts. On the flight home, once they were in the air, they made love one more time at thirty thousand feet over paradise, promising to return soon.

Charles and Giselle are ready to get married. Giselle lost all her baby weight, so she can fit into the beautiful gown she picked out. Her mom flew in from New Orleans early to help with last-minute details, and her dad flew out the night before the wedding. Since Giselle doesn't have many friends in Vegas, most of the guests were their usual circle, family, Charles' close friends, and parents. Their wedding was small, with about fifty people attending, because they wanted to keep it simple.

Charles spent quite a bit on Giselle's ring and the wedding combined, and he pays all the household bills, so money is kind of tight for them right now. He saved as much as he could, but the cost of the honeymoon nearly broke the bank. As a wedding gift, Art provided them with the full use of his jet, which came in very handy, and they were appreciative. Art has always been fond of Charles, and he had no ill feelings towards him because of Veronica's poor decisions. Having the opportunity to make their honeymoon more convenient was a no brainer.

Giselle decided to have all the girls at the wedding, and they were the delight of every guest. Their baby girl Mina Corinne sat with her Yaya (Giselle's mom) to watch her parents marry. Art and Sofia had their event planner set up the yard for another incredible wedding, full of flowers, white linen tablecloths, lots of great food, drinks, and delicious wedding cake. Their wedding went off without a hitch, and as promised, Art flew them out to Maui for a week. Since Leilani has a live-in babysitter, plus the twins Zara and Zoe to help, she offered to keep Mina Corinne so they could enjoy themselves.

When Charles and Giselle boarded the plane, Art had everything nicely set up with food and beverages and envelopes placed on their seats. Inside their envelopes were five thousand dollars in cash each, with a note saying congratulations and enjoy! Art's kindness and generosity genuinely touch Charles. He smiles and kisses his bride. With the hotel paid for and the flight is taken care of by Art, they had all the money they needed to have a great time in the Valley Isle of Maui. Their Club Oceanview suite at the Four Seasons Maui at Wailea felt magical from the moment they arrived. Their beautiful suite has high ceilings, and spacious lanais that overlook the ocean, with textures and art inspired patterns of the Wailea coastline.

During the day, they went to O'O Farms for a farm to table feast and hung out on the north shore to join the community and shopped. They took a sunset cruise and partied at a traditional Luau enjoying great food great stories, and were mesmerized by the line of Kane and hula dancers. They rented a jeep and drove the Road to Hana packed with waterfalls, canyons, rocky beaches, rainforests, swimming holes, and unique roadside stands. They toured the Botanical Gardens with Giselle taking selfies and videos of the two of them every step of the way.

148

A couple's massage was first on their things to do during the day, and later, they explored the town for lunch. At the end of their evenings, they stargazed on the beach each night before returning to their suite. At the end of each full and exciting day, they retreated to their room and passionately loved each other, cherishing every moment of their alone time. Charles and Giselle have a very satisfying intimate life, but they kicked it up a few notches on their honeymoon retreat. As their relaxing getaway sadly came to its end, sleeping on the plane during their return home was their best option.

The twins Zara and Zoe are doing well working at the daycare and take care of their nieces Issa, Kaira, and Arabella two days a week. A publication that focuses on local businesses, and corporations scheduled an interview to do a photoshoot at the center. Hank's twin sisters are gorgeous, with deep dark complexions who resemble the Australian Super Model Duckie Thot. His twin daughters are also identical and beautiful but have a lighter, caramel complexion and are starting to favor his sisters more each day. When the interviewer and camera crew arrived, both sets of twins immediately caught their attention, so with permission, the interviewer directed the team to start taking candid photos of them. Just then, Arabella skipped into the room, flashing her bright, blue eyes with her bouncing Shirley Temple curls of hair straight into Zara's arms. Once the interviewer saw her, she quickly motioned to her camera guy to photograph her as well. All five of these girls are beautiful, and her photographer captures some great shots of them all.

When the magazine spread came out, all the girls were on the cover as their featured story. This publication is circulated all over the valley, and that cover and inside story got the right people's attention. Several other publications wanted to know who the girls were. An agent contacted Leilani to enquire if she would be interested in having the girls do some modeling for some of her advertising clients. She talked it over with Hank and Art, and they all agreed that it would be ok for a while.

One week later, the girls booked another photoshoot for a clothing boutique in Town Square and a spread for a hair salon in Summerlin. Soon their faces were in more print ads as their look began to be more in demand. A few malls displayed larger than life photos of them in various store windows, and the money started pouring in. Their agent's business expanded so well because of their gigs, she started booking them outside of Las Vegas, and once again, Art's plane came in handy. Zoe and Zara secured a gig with a national clothing brand, and the younger twins, Issa and Kaira, landed their likeness on a National brand of diapers, which usually stays on the brand for decades. Now their new normal; Art, Hank, and Leilani take turns traveling with the girls for gigs all over the country.

With gigs coming in more frequently, grossing over ten thousand dollars a month each for Zara and Zoe, they quit their jobs at the center. They loved working with all the kids and learned much more than they expected. They are also grateful to Leilani for giving them a good start in Vegas, and Hank and their parents could not be happier. Now that Arabella is in school, her gigs are less frequent, but she still earns tens of thousands of dollars every month. Taking piano lessons, learning Spanish from the nanny, and French and Italian from her dad keeps her quite busy. Listening to her practice on the piano, Art is pleased with how beautiful and bright she is. Tearing up, he wishes Philippe and his parents were here to know her. Just then, Sofia walks in from her doctor's appointment, kissed his face, and told him the good news that they are having a boy, and he could not be happier.

Veronica being alone in Colorado got bored and decided to return to Vegas so she can figure out what she's going to do with her life. She doesn't have a job, and she's only going to get ten percent of the cannabis profits each month. Right now, it's not enough for her to live on, so she wants to talk with Art to see if he is open to revisions. When she arrived at Art's house and walked in, she watched Sofia walking down the stairs, sporting her baby bump. After saying hello, Sofia wanted to know from Veronica if she found a place to live yet. Apologizing, Veronica told her no but quickly said Art told her she could stay until she found a home. Sofia then said, "Well, that was before I became his wife, and since our family is growing, it's time for you to go." Shocked and feeling devastated, Veronica could not believe what Sofia just said to her.

Just then, Art walked in, hugged and kissed Sofia, and greeted Veronica. Making small talk, he asked how things went in Colorado. "Great, can I speak with you for a moment?". Sofia then abruptly interjected and said, "Yes, let's talk, Veronica." Baffled, confused, and caught off guard, Veronica looked at Art wide-eyed and continued to direct her comments towards him, which made Sofia angry, so this time Sofia snapped at Veronica. Wanting to defuse the situation, Art put his hand on Sofia's shoulder to calm her down and encouraged Veronica to speak up and say whatever she needed to say. Veronica hesitantly told Art that the ten percent she is due to receive from the farm profits might not be enough for her to find the right home to live in to start a new life.

Immediately like a barracuda, Sofia jumped right back in and looked Veronica directly in her face, and said, if you're having trouble finding a place to live, why don't you ask if Leilani will let you stay at her center?! That way, you won't be close to being homeless, like you tried to make Leilani when you kicked her out of this house! Veronica was shocked and could not stop the tears from falling down her face as Sofia continued to taunt her. "Yeah, you didn't think I knew about all of that, did you?" Then Sofia said, "I can't even believe Art allows you to still live in this house after what you did to her!" Art intervened and calmed Sofia down, and she stormed off into the kitchen. In a low voice, Art told Veronica not to worry, that he'll figure something out, and Veronica said ok, thank you. She walked away and went up to her room, feeling like this was just a horrible nightmare.

Art joined Sofia in the kitchen, and he can see that she is upset. Knowing what Veronica did to Leilani not only makes her sad, but it makes her angry as well. Art feels somewhat torn and wished Sofia didn't know about it, but it is what it is. Art is surprised that Sofia even knew as much as she did, but he tried his best to get her to remain calm. Sofia very

152

emotionally asked Art how he would feel if Veronica had done that to her? He replied, saying, "That girl worked for me over ten years and helped me make a lot of money." Then Sofia said, "But babe, she took your money and Leilani's, so how can you even trust her"? Art replied, "Well, you're right, she did take some of my money, but not all of it. She didn't touch the money in my bank accounts. Don't worry, babe, the ninety million in those accounts are steadily growing, and we will all be ok. Now let's go out and have a nice dinner and enjoy the evening", as he gently grabbed her face with both his hands and kissed her lips. "Ok, Sofia said, but she needs to get out of this house soon." "Ok, my love, you got it, now let's go."

Once the two of them left the house, Veronica went downstairs to get a drink and had way more than she should have. Trying to figure out what she's going to do, her thoughts are cluttered, and the booze effects aren't helping. Feeling claustrophobic, Veronica jumped in her car for a drive to clear her head in the night air. As she entered onto the freeway, a wrong-way driver hit her head-on. After the crash, the other car plummeted into the air, flipped three times, and landed about fifty feet away from hers, causing him to die instantly. Veronica, obviously shaken and in pain from multiple broken bones, fell unconscious until the emergency rescue vehicles arrive. Trapped inside, the paramedics removed her from the entangled car and rushed her to the hospital. Because she wreaked of alcohol, they immediately tested her upon arrival at the hospital. Because the other driver died, they could not readily access who was at fault. Veronica's blood-alcohol level was three times over the legal limit, so at the very least, she will be charged with a DUI. Along with broken bones, she also suffered from several internal injuries, including a concussion, but was soon stabilized.

She lay in the hospital covered with bandages connected to tubes, with monitors beeping, mostly sleeping from heavy meds. Charles and Art have always been her emergency contact, so Art was surprised to see her that way when he walked in. Two detectives were speaking with her about the accident, so he stood there and listened. Unfortunately, Veronica didn't remember anything, so they started filling in the blanks, telling her; both cars were totaled, she was drunk, and the other driver did not survive the crash. Starting to panic at what they were saying, her vitals began to rise. Art summoned a nurse. The nurse quickly intervened, attended to Veronica, and told the detectives to come back later. After hearing what those detectives were telling her, Art was concerned. Looking at the fear in her eyes, he leaned over real close and spoke softly, asking her what she remembers, and she told him she remembers nothing. Art has never known Veronica to drink excessively, so his first instinct is to help her. He told her not to worry and concentrate on getting better, and he will help her. He feels terrible, but he's also struggling with how much he should help her financially to beat this case.

Veronica spent several weeks recovering, and afterward, she transferred to rehab on a different floor of the hospital. She was allowed to continue rehab only because the coroner reported that the other driver was also over the legal limit. That required the investigators to put more effort into solving out who was at fault. Going straight to rehab allowed Veronica more time to recover from her injuries. It also gave her time to obtain a competent legal defense without being arrested and thrown in jail for a homicidal DUI. Art is close with the Police Chief, so he called in a favor.

Her memory is starting to come back and tries to tell Art about what she thought happened when he visits her, but she is not entirely sure. The trauma of all her injuries, plus the fact that a person died, takes its toll on her, so she is very depressed. She told him she might have gotten on the wrong freeway ramp because all she saw coming were lights, and she doesn't remember anything after that. Art quickly hushed her and told her how the story would go. He told her to tell the detectives that the other guy was going the wrong way, and before she could do anything, the crash just happened, and she said ok. Art told Veronica the other guy was drunk.

Meanwhile, two months later, Sofia went into labor, and finally, after eight hours, she gave birth to Luka Philippe Graziani. A beautiful seven-pound, eight-ounce, healthy baby boy with lots of dark curly hair and a great set of lungs. Sofia and Art both cried tears of joy as they doted over their bundle of joy and couldn't be more excited. The group is all excited about Art and Sofia having a baby boy, and they all welcome him with lots of gifts. Arabella is incredibly happy about having a baby brother to play with along with her twin sisters.

Now with so many children in the group, Tony feels the fatherhood itch and wants to set a date so he and Isabella can get married. He wants to be married before they have kids, so he would like to get married sooner than later. He found a reasonably priced house and moved from Leilani and Hanks home before he and Isabella decided to elope secretly. When they returned, Isabella and Gabriella moved in with Tony as his new family.

By the time Veronica gets discharged from rehab, she's left owing thousands of dollars, but sadly, she has no way to pay for it. She has no money, no car, and no place to live. Sofia does not want her living in the house with them, so Art contemplates what to do for her. He thought about suggesting she reach out to her foster dad about moving back to Cleveland, but he's not sure if she would want to do that. Again, Sofia suggests that Veronica should ask Leilani if she can live at the center. After all, it is a place that helps women who have housing issues. It would be easy for Art to get her set up in a little place to get on her feet, get a job, and take care of herself, but Sofia is totally against anything like that.

Sofia feels that Veronica was entirely too greedy to do what she did to Leilani, and she should figure out on her own how to fix it. Art knew Veronica could only go downhill, so he secretly gave her a thousand dollars and told her to get a cheap room in a hotel just for now, and he will see what he can do. She asked him if she could maybe stay in one of his Santa Monica condo's, but Art told her no because Sofia handles all the rentals, and she would never go for it. Feeling hopeless, Veronica couldn't believe her life has come to this. She took an Uber to the cheapest hotel she could find and cried herself to sleep.

When Veronica woke up the next morning, her mind was clear. She reached for her cell phone and read a text message from the detective saying he needs to meet with her tomorrow at 2:30. Taking in a deep breath, at this point, Veronica knew what to do. She called Leilani's center and asked if she could move in. Art had already contacted Leilani and discussed it with her, so the intake administrator was waiting for Veronica's call and told her, "Yes, we have one opening, and you can come in as soon as tomorrow." Leilani's heart is Fpure and without hatred or envy, so of course, she would do whatever she could to help. When Veronica arrived at the center, the admission staff went over all the rules and regulations required to sign and admitted her.

Veronica roommates with another woman who also has no children, and they explained since she has no income, she can work on property to fulfill her obligation of paying the rent. She can either work at the daycare, the job resource training dept, the kitchen, or janitorial work. The rental agreement is only ten percent of residents' wages, designed to help them get on their feet to secure a place of their own eventually. Feeling at her worse and being reduced to such an embarrassing level, she asked to work in the job resource department.

Veronica Feels this place is just two steps above being in jail, except it's just cleaner. She must agree to all the terms, and if she breaks any of the rules, she gets evicted, no questions asked. Veronica took a deep breath and signed on the dotted line, vowing to give herself thirty days to get out one way or the other. The administrator walked her over to her assigned unit, and she met her roommate. She seemed nice enough as they casually chatted, and Veronica was happy that she wasn't homeless. The room was modestly furnished, with two twin beds, a nightstand, a lamp, and a dresser.

She's allowed to decorate it any way she wants but plans to be there for no more than thirty days.

For now, she is preparing her mind for where she might spend the rest of her life. She has to meet with the detective later that afternoon, and she is scared shitless. Feeling hopelessly alone with no one to turn to, she thought about Art. The one person she trusted the most feels like a world away, and she wonders if he will even help her with this unfortunate situation. She picked up her phone to call him just to talk and get some moral support, but he didn't answer.

Feeling hopeless, sitting in her bleak and depressing room at the center, Veronica can't believe this is the beginning of her ultimate fate. As Karma would have it, the nightmare of her future lasted much more than thirty days. Art and Sofia are home enjoying their beautiful baby boy Luka. He is the light of their lives as their family comes full circle. Art is so happy; he stares at his beautiful family, thinking he must have done something right in life to be this blessed.

Until Next Season